WHEN YOU LEAVE

MONICA ROPAL

RP|TEENS
PHILADELPHIA · LONDON

Books published by Running Press are available at special discounts for
bulk purchases in the United States by corporations, institutions, and
other organizations. For more information, please contact the Special
Markets Department at the Perseus Books Group, 2300 Chestnut Street,
Suite 200, Philadelphia, PA 19103, or call (800) 810-4145, ext. 5000, or
e-mail special.markets@perseusbooks.com.

ISBN 978-0-7624-5455-6
Library of Congress Control Number: 2015930499
E-book ISBN 978-0-7624-5630-7

9 8 7 6 5 4 3 2 1
Digit on the right indicates the number of this printing

Designed by T.L. Bonaddio
Cover art by T.L. Bonaddio
Edited by Marlo Scrimizzi
Typography: Museo Sans, Calligraffiti, Bell MT,
Bell Gothic, and Juri Handwriting

Published by Running Press Teens
An Imprint of Running Press Book Publishers
A Member of the Perseus Books Group
2300 Chestnut Street
Philadelphia, PA 19103–4371

Visit us on the web!
www.runningpress.com/rpkids

FOR WYATT, NICK, AND ALICE.

Dream Big. Love Large. Find Happy.

Chapter 1

I fought the tickle, my nose to the blackboard, stifling the urge to sneeze.

Old school detention was medieval. It would be a slow cruel death of boredom. Under my uniform skirt my knees bobbed. I glanced down to where my bag was flopped open on the floor next to me. I could see the inside pocket that held my phone. It would take me twenty seconds tops to text Mattie. He'd give me a thumb lashing for getting in bad with the Sister again, but any communication would help dash away the quiet in the empty room and calm the noise in my brain.

I let my forehead roll against the cool slate.

Only three weeks into my three-year sentence at St. Bernadette's, and already I was on the brink of a rep with Sister Rita for my attitude. The plan was to have no rep at all, to suffer through in anonymity in my long blonde hair and just-like-everyone-else uniform. I'd even gone as far as straightening my slouch and sitting pretty with my knees close together to appear like a girl who belongs at a private school, instead of a skater girl who didn't.

I thought of Mattie again. Even with his ten-minute skate ride from Kellogg Senior High, he'd be out there waiting. I'd barely flexed my fingers to reach for my phone, when the door clicked open, causing me to snap to attention.

Footsteps moved behind me. Those tapping footsteps didn't belong to Sister Rita's clodhoppers, and neither did the musky cologne that overpowered the smell of chalk.

Drawers slid open and closed. Nothing like the controlled movements of Sister Rita.

I braved a full turn around. There, with his back to me, was Cooper McCay standing at Sister's desk, hand still gripped on the open drawer to his left. Cooper's locker was two down from mine, but our social statuses were on entirely different planes. He was part of a loud, obnoxious, in-love-with-themselves trio of guys that had girls wetting themselves at every smile tossed their way.

Typical pretty boy. Except some things about him weren't. Like how he'd get easily bored by the fawning cheerleaders or emit the occasional irritated sigh in the wake of his buddies' foolishness. I'll admit to finding him more . . . interesting than the average St. B pretty boy.

I took the opportunity to admire the strong line where his neck met the width of his shoulder. Not to mention other pleasing attributes that this view allowed. There was something about a good pair of khakis on a nice—

"Getting an eyeful, newbie?" he asked, pausing in his search, unruffled by my staring at him.

"It's Cass," I blurted out. Not even sure why. I usually wasn't one for sharing. "Does Sister Rita know you're going through her desk?"

He shrugged. "Maybe I'm the new cleaning staff?"

"And maybe you're trying to steal her rosary."

"Well, Cass, maybe—"

There were voices in the hall and I swung around toward the door, realizing we were about to be found out. I heard Cooper bump the edge of Sister Rita's desk. In three long strides his arm was around me, pulling me toward him. Before I could blink, his lips were on mine. It could only have been sudden insanity that had me going along and not kneeing him in the balls.

"Mister McCay!" Sister Rita drew out the *s*, hissing her dismay.

He pulled away. His arm loosened its grip and my weak knees threatened to leave me puddled on the floor. And I'm not the kind to puddle. I rubbed my hand over my arm to smooth away the goose bumps.

Sister Rita looked as if her eyes might make a leap right over her reading glasses. She ran a hand over the cross hanging in the front of her blue sweater.

Cooper touched the back of his hand to his mouth. "Sorry. I was just about to go meet my father when I saw my girlfriend in here." He paused to flash that crooked smile. "How embarrassing."

He was either crazy, or a genius, or both. But embarrassed? Not.

Sister Rita's eyes were nearly as big as mine as her head jerked from him to me and back to him.

"I wasn't aware that you and Miss . . ." She trailed off as if placing us both in the same sentence was beyond her. She settled at narrowing her eyes.

He tipped his head in conspiracy. "Well, it's sort of on the down low. Seeing as we come from such . . . different . . . families and all."

He rubbed the back of his neck with his hand, dodging a quick glance in my direction. Funny that he'd get all fidgety when it came to the truth of it.

"I see." She looked over to me again, then her eyes

flicked back to Cooper. Her left eyebrow arched. "Did you say your father was waiting for you?"

Either Cooper's dad had some pull in this school or maybe she simply didn't want to deal with the two of us, scandalizing as we were. Ha.

Sister Rita sat down at her desk, her attention turning to a stack of papers. "You are dismissed," she said without looking back up.

Cooper picked up my bag and slung the strap over his shoulder. He held out his hand.

"Ready, Cass?" he asked.

Hell yes. Genius. Loved it. I took his hand and let him lead me out.

I know when I'm being used. But I never count it as being used if it's mutually beneficial in some way.

The classroom door shut behind us. We couldn't even make it ten steps before releasing the laughter we were holding. When his gaze lingered on me, the laughter dried and I pulled my hand from his.

I glanced around, but didn't see anyone in the hall. Another two classrooms and we'd reached our row of lockers. I worked my lock and tried to avoid eye contact with Cooper as he slouched against his locker only inches away from me.

"Thanks. I needed a reason to explain why I was there," Cooper said.

I shrugged. "I figured it was that. That . . . that was

the thing." I took a breath to school my emotions as the lock clicked open. All my friends were guys. Guys did not make me nervous. Usually.

Cooper rubbed the back of his neck again. "Yeah . . . ," he said under his breath.

I heard a noise by the stairs, but when I checked around again, no one was there. "What were you looking for in Sister Rita's desk?" I asked in a low voice, and grabbed my French text off the top shelf.

"She confiscated a girl's iPod in second period. I told her I'd try to get it back for her."

A girl. Figures. Then I remembered I didn't care. "Whatevs. You got me out of detention early, so we're even."

"Yeah," he said again. His body was already half turned, but his shoulders seemed to be shifting back and forth with physical indecision about whether to stay or bail.

I slammed the locker door and tucked the textbook under my arm. It was time to make the decision for him before he started getting any funny ideas.

"This never happened."

Chapter 2

I turned away from Cooper and made my way to the art hallway at the back of the school, my daily incognito escape route. I hurried past the pottery room, glancing over as the kiln in the back *whooshed*—the fire hardening the day's collection of bowls and ashtrays.

The fact that I had to shake my hands to rid my body of the rigid adrenaline was freaking me out. It was just a kiss. It didn't mean anything.

I pushed through the exit door at the end of the hall and closed my eyes as the cold blast of air hit my warm cheeks. There was no lingering Minnesota summer humidity this year. I was sure we'd be seeing snow by Halloween.

I stepped out onto the loading dock and looked down at Mattie perched on the edge. His skateboard was next to him on his right, mine to his left. Even in fifty degrees he was already in a sweat, which told me he'd been having a skateboard sesh without me. His six-foot, skinny frame was folded up. Even with sweaty hair his cowlick refused to lie flat. I combed it down with my hand.

He tapped his watch with his finger twice.

You're late.

It had been nine years since cancer surgery took Mattie's voice. But without a glitch, I continued to hear him—only inside my head instead of through my ears. After growing up with him, every quirk of a brow and shrug of a shoulder spoke to me. Since he's a guy, it's possible I get more words out of him now than I did before.

I shifted my weight. "I know I'm late. Sister Rita—"

He hopped to his feet, throwing his gorilla arms out wide. *Again?*

"She has it out for me."

He wiped his fingers across my forehead. *Chalk.*

"See? Medieval."

I heard the door creak behind me and whipped around to see Cooper stepping through.

He glanced over at Mattie, and then back to me. My cheeks were feeling that long-lost August humidity.

Cooper held out my bag. "You forgot this. In detention."

14

I glanced down at myself. Of course it wasn't there. I stepped forward and grabbed my bag without looking at him. "Thanks," I said, but in a whisper because I had forgotten to breathe. I stared at my bag, not daring to look at Mattie.

Out of the corner of my eye, I saw Cooper turning back the way he came, until Mattie snapped his fingers.

Mattie wasn't working at getting my attention, he was looking at Cooper. Mattie pointed at him and indicated his own face. I shot a look at Cooper and saw what Mattie was talking about. Cooper had the faint remains of chalk dust—my chalk dust—on his left cheek and forehead.

Cooper wiped it away with his sleeve. "Thanks. Sister Rita's chalkboard needs some cleaning." His eyes went to mine for a second, and then he pulled open the door and went back inside, leaving Mattie and me in silence.

Mattie raised his eyebrows at me.

"As if," I said, and left it at that.

Really? He asked with a tip of his head.

"It's nothing. It never even happened."

"It" what?

"Drop it. I have a skate park to thrash." I waited to see if he was going to interrogate me, but when he started kicking chips of loose cement over the edge into the parking lot, I figured he must be over it . . . or not interested . . . or biding his time to use it against me.

I took the steps down to the uneven blacktop, then moved behind Dumpsters along the brick wall. I heard Mattie's shoes smack as he jumped down instead of using the stairs. I tried to ignore the smells of rotting carpet and glue coming from the Dumpsters as I pulled out the change of clothes from my bag.

"Sister Rita does have it out for me, though," I said, pulling my pants over my tights.

I peeked around to see Mattie feigning a yawn.

"It's true." Pants buttoned, I unhooked the skirt. "You'd think slouching was a capital offense—what?"

His shoulders were doing their bounce of silent laughter. He shook his head at me.

You did not.

"No, I didn't get detention for slouching. I'm just saying. I don't know what I did wrong. Move and breathe? I swear the woman hates everything about me." I started to unbutton my shirt.

Oh, Cass, you roll me.

He was the first to call me Cass. Not "Cassie" like my parents, or "Cassandra" like Grandma Rossi or Sister Rita. Just Cass.

When I got to the final button I realized his shoulders had stilled and his eyes were fixed.

"Mattie you have two seconds to turn your fat face before I break it."

He turned, but there went the shoulders again.

I changed my shirt, zipped on my hoodie, and tied my hair in a knot. It wasn't that he'd never seen me in a sports bra. He'd no doubt seen me in less over the years of friendship that had sprouted in toddlerhood. But it was only recently that there was anything there to see. I'm what you'd call a late bloomer.

"Go ahead and laugh, but let me remind you, I did not even let out a single giggle when you started shaving—yes, I noticed—or when I found those dirty mags in your—"

He clamped a hand over my mouth and rested his forehead against my temple.

I'm sorry.

And I knew he was. Mattie never lied to me. But I never claimed to be as good as him.

He pulled away and stomped the tail of my board, catching it midair, before handing it over.

Two more taps on his watch. *We're late.*

Chapter 3

Gav and Franklin were already at the skate park when we arrived. Franklin was working on rails in the Street Plaza and Gav was on the half pipe—hard to miss with his lock of black hair dyed fluorescent green to match the bottom of his board. I pulled on my helmet and pads and watched him do a series of frontside early grabs. That boy could do frontside early grabs forever. He didn't care a lot for tricks. But me? If I don't land a tre flip this year I might not be able to skate anymore. I waited for his last axle stall and dropped in right next to him.

I'm kidding about the tre flip. Sort of. I'd become more competitive lately. If I'm not hitting it hard and working up a sweat, then I'm not doing it right. I wanted to leave the pipe exhausted. Wrung out. Thoughtless. I loved the physicality of skating. I loved getting my mind and body in sync with something amazing. And I loved that when the boys and I were out together, skating was ours. We owned it.

But thirty seconds after dropping in, Cooper was on my mind and my wheel hit the coping. I slid down on my knee pads.

Gav came to join me as I sulked in the grass. "What's up with the sucking today?" he said. "You were way closer to nailing it a week ago."

"Not feeling it today."

"Did something happen?"

"Why would something need to happen? I'm just not feeling it."

He laughed. "You think you have it all nailed down, but I know you. You wear your heart on your sleeve when you skate. I see you." Gav was the unofficial caretaker of the group. Always checking in. Always trying to get us to open up.

"What do you see, idiot?" I said, swinging my arm around his neck, ignoring the slick of sweat from his hair on my skin.

"Something has changed."

I took too long to answer. Because I didn't know the answer. No, I did know. "Nothing has changed. I'm here. I'm going to kill that tre flip before it kills me."

×

The next day I managed to dodge Cooper's occasional glances by stifling my own ill-timed glances. I told myself to knock it off.

After school I sat on the bench next to Mattie at the bus stop across from my school. We were waiting for the 63B bus to take us up to Rosedale Mall. Our buddy Franklin knew some girl from Kellogg High who could get us free sub sandwiches when she was working. With his American Indian/something exotic ethnicity, Franklin was the kind of attractive that always had some girl willing to get us some thing. Gav was supposed to meet us, too, but had apparently made some excuse to Franklin about being late.

I thought of Cooper again, and the way his eyes would move to mine when we were both at our lockers, and how it made my heart beat fast. Even now, thinking about it was affecting me. Aware of Mattie's knee bouncing next to mine, I shook off my thoughts of Cooper and glanced at my watch. Six minutes until the next bus. Franklin's too-loud-for-public voice was rattling on about the sandwich chick and how her boobs were as big as—

"This chick better have sandwiches as big as her tits," I said, cutting him off. "I'm starving."

Franklin slapped his leg. "Damn! Sounds like the perfect woman. Big sandwiches and titties. Am I right, Mattie?" Franklin laughed, not waiting for Mattie to answer.

Franklin was tall, like Mattie. But where Mattie had the makings of some kind of build going on, Franklin was just a bag of bones. He looked like straight up and down six o'clock. His dark arms stretched out dramatically, letting out a yawn that was more like a moaning yowl, causing a lady in a business suit to edge farther down the sidewalk away from us. Idiot.

Mattie's knee stilled and I glanced over at him. He was squinting with his gaze across the street, on the fence that lined the grounds of St. Bernadette's. I was about to question him when I saw it for myself.

Gav, as usual, was hard to miss among the lingering uniforms that lined the sidewalk in front of my school. He wore his black Windbreaker lined with fluorescent green piping, matching the lock of hair. Hard to miss.

I opened my mouth, but Franklin was already calling out to him. Gav didn't seem to hear him across the traffic. Instead of looking for us, he was chatting with a tall brown-haired girl. Weird because Gav wasn't generally into brunettes, and weirder because he wasn't at all into girls.

"Who dat girlie?" Franklin mumbled under his breath.

We watched Gav for a minute, shooting the breeze with this stranger, and I glanced again at my watch. Two minutes. My phone buzzed and I heard Franklin's alert tone next to me.

Should I get him? Mattie had texted, now standing.

Behind Gav, two guys stepped through the school gates onto the sidewalk. One was a shorter African-American-looking guy, the other a taller brown-haired white guy. Both built thick like footballers. As soon as they saw Gav with the brunette girlie, they went straight for him. I sucked in a breath as the bigger one shoved Gav from behind, causing him to lose his footing. I stood up and toed the curb. Those guys . . . they were Cooper's friends who rounded out the popular trio. I scanned the space that was visible through the gates—without any sign of Cooper—and looked back to Gav.

Even the shorter one, who I think was called Eli, had a foot on Gav, not to mention fifty pounds of muscle. Devon, the taller one, was yelling with a finger pointed in Gav's face. I was still processing when the movement started around me. Franklin and Mattie were off the curb and edging forward, barely waiting for a break in traffic. I reached out for their arms. I tried to simultaneously calculate the level of danger Gav was in, while making sure Mattie and Franklin didn't get themselves creamed by the heavy traffic on Snelling Avenue.

"Wait," I said.

The St. B's guys were backing off. Gav looked across to us, giving a single nod of reassurance, before dropping his board down and riding toward the intersection as the light turned green for him to cross. Franklin jogged over to meet him halfway on the crosswalk. I jerked the back of Mattie's hoodie to get him back up on the curb as a Lincoln rolled by and nearly shined Mattie's shoes with its tires.

We boarded the bus together and paid our fare in line. The driver grunted at us. Franklin and Gav plopped down in the sideways bench behind the driver, and Mattie edged over in the first row on Gav's right, and I dropped in next to Mattie.

"You okay?" I said to Gav, leaning forward. "What was up with those guys?"

Gav stood up and stuffed his wallet in his back pocket. He took his time shaking out his legs and rolling his neck. Gav was ADHD, so answers would come whenever he and his body were ready. "Typical shit. Skater haters, you know."

The bus jerked as it started off again. I looked out the window across Mattie and my heart jumped as I saw Cooper with Devon and Eli. Mattie was eyeing me sideways, but he didn't say anything.

Franklin was also staring out the window. "Assholes. All of them. Steer your brilliant mind clear of that lot, Cass."

I stiffened and dropped my gaze to Gav's board. The wheels were Racers brand. High end, big buck. Gav and the boys live in the Frogtown area of St. Paul.

Frogtown boys. Frogtown, though only a handful of miles from the hipster area of St. B's, might as well be another planet. High crime, low income. Bulletproof windows around the cashiers at the gas stations and off-duty cops at the grocery.

Gav and his sister, Greta, live mostly with their mom who got by on welfare and child support, which they never saw the results of. He never had anything that wasn't charity, borrowed, or stolen. I should know because up until we moved in with my step-dad, Mom and I lived two doors down from Gav. Our mothers were constantly comparing notes on who was giving away what. I remember being in kinder-garten and Gav's mom and dad sharing food stamps and WIC coupons with us, or us with them, depend-ing on who was having a better month. Of course, all that changed when Mom remarried. Now we ate steak once a week, had a TV in every room, and Mom acted like she didn't know Gav when he came over. As I opened my mouth to ask Gav about the new wheels, Franklin broke in.

"Those guys are all about ego. They think they can shit on us. Just like Decker at Harding, jumping us every chance he got."

My stomach turned at the thought. In junior high, Vaughn Decker and his buds made it their hobby to beat on the boys, and talk a mile to me when they caught any of us out alone. They broke Gav's arm one day after school. Cops believed their story that it was an accident, and never even bothered to press charges or generally just give a damn. Luckily, Decker moved away shortly after that or Franklin might have made good on all his chat about street justice. But this wasn't like that. Cooper wasn't like that.

Franklin was still going off. "If they think they can just disrespect us 'cause we're skaters, they're gonna have another thing coming. Am I right?"

I really hated when Franklin asked "Am I right?" like we all had to agree with him about everything. Mattie's knee budged into mine and I realized Franklin was staring at me.

"Swear to God, Cass, you can make out with every guy at the Aquatennial Skate Fair next summer—"

"Again," Gav said with a smile.

"—just don't fall for any of those losers," Franklin said.

I looked at Gav who was barely holding back his laughter. I felt the smile spread across my face. "Excuse me. There was one guy at the skate fair."

"You got the numbers of, like, three others!" Gav said.

"Please. There were only two other skater girls at the entire fair and, like, a hundred guys. Could've gotten more."

Mattie's shoulders were going.

"You probably got more numbers than me, Gav," I said.

"True. I got mad game."

Next to him Franklin's green eyes were still drilling into me from behind his dark bangs. He was taking my disregard for his statement as mutiny. His eyes glided over to Mattie. Had Mattie given something away?

I spoke up to get Franklin's attention back on me. "Don't worry. I'm not at that school to make friends, especially with guys like that."

Chapter 4

On Thursday I was still trying hard, but failing badly, at dodging eye contact with Cooper. Something was different, and it took me until midmorning to realize what it was. He'd been smiling at me. Smiling made me nervous. If the kiss never happened, there was no reason for smiling.

At first I thought it was my imagination. I kept my head down as I approached my locker between second and third period trying to think what I needed, with the usual chaos thundering around me in the hall. Cooper was whispering to someone standing between us. I glanced just for a second and could see the framing of brown hair and wide brown eyes simpering up at Cooper on his other side. She looked like Gav's girlie from outside the school.

"It's just between us, right? I don't want anyone else to know," she said to Cooper.

I froze in place. Some chirpy girls walked behind us and I missed whatever he said back to her. Whatever it was must have satisfied her because the brunette moved around me.

"I'll meet you tomorrow," she called over her shoulder, and down the hall she went. I realized I wasn't moving, and felt Cooper's stillness, too. We both were just standing there breathing. I couldn't help but turn my head. As soon as I could capture his lips curling upward, a crash behind us caused me to turn. A tall guy with black rimmed glasses had spilled over a heap of books at his locker across the way. Someone laughed and Black Glasses gave him a one-handed shove.

When I looked back, Cooper was joined by Eli and Devon and some little blonde thing Devon had his arm around. They made their way down the hall toward the stairs. Cooper didn't look back. As I watched the back of his head move through the crowd, the anger itched up my neck.

Between third and fourth period, I thought about avoiding my locker all together, but fourth period was Sister Rita, and if I was going to get the A in Ethics that she was trying to rob me of, I couldn't miss a single assignment. My paper on the Tuskegee experiment (and how it was all kinds of wrong) was still in my locker.

Once again, Cooper was there at his locker and he was smiling at me. I could feel it. It was pissing me off, all that smiling. What the hell was he thinking? Was it some kind of joke? I blocked him out so I could connect my brain back with what my hands were doing, because all that smiling was making me think about his lips, and thinking about his lips made me think about the kiss, and thinking about the kiss made multitasking impossible.

I grabbed my green Ethics folder and slammed my locker door.

The crowd was thinning out around us because the bell was about to ring. I could feel it. And that hacked me off even more. He'd made me late with all this smiling.

I turned to face him. He was leaning, all casual, with a damn smirk on his face. He flipped his blond hair off his face and opened his mouth to no doubt say something witty or inviting.

I held up a finger. "Stop smiling at me."

I watched the edges of his lips droop. I watched the emotions flit past his eyes. I realized I'd been watching too long when the bell rang above us. I walked away, remembering not to look back. And then I remembered to breathe.

×

Last period was breaking up. I sat on my hard metal stool, staring at the canvas in front of me. The art rooms were one large room broken up by shelves and tables and partitions dividing pottery from jewelry, life drawing, and painting.

Painting was the closest to the hall, and farthest from Mr. Sandreski's office. He was cool about us lingering after period if we hadn't "expelled all our creative energy" for the day.

I stared at the empty boat in the lake on my canvas which was supposed to capture a "summer dream." But instead of looking like Camp Sunshine, the lake had somehow turned into a murky Loch Ness.

I'd cooled down since this morning. It was stupid to get so angry. It was nothing.

I took my canvas over to the drying racks and slid mine in, went back for my paint tray and brought it over to the sink. I was tossing my brush into the cubby with my name on it, when I heard someone behind me.

"Cass."

Cooper was at the door. Not in, not out, and lucky for him, not leaning or smirking.

"Hey. Sorry about the smiling," he said.

I shrugged, or tried, but the muscles were tight and did more of a stiff twitch. "Forgiven. Since we aren't supposed to have met, your apology isn't necessary. But neither is the smiling. Which was kind of the point."

He nodded.

I wiped my wet hands on my uniform skirt, then went back to gather my stuff and put on my sweater. I pulled the long strap of my bag over my head. I purposefully took time adjusting it, giving him plenty of time to vacate.

He was still waiting at the door.

"Do me a favor," I said. "Not to be harsh, but I was serious about the other day never happening. I'm getting by as background scenery here, which is how I like it." I double-checked the clasps on my bag to avoid looking at him.

"So you're probably going to say no when I invite you over to my house?"

I nearly pulled a tendon in the side of my neck to look at him.

"No, no, no. Not like that." He held up his hands. "Just wondering if you want to hang out. Just . . . hang out? Not necessarily at my house. Anywhere you want, really." Was that a blush?

I swallowed. Pretty boys at St. B's did not blush. Even ones with crooked smiles and bumpy noses—and was that a scar on his bottom lip?

I shook my head to clear it. "Hang out? I don't even know what that would look like."

He laughed, but seemed to catch on that I was serious. "It might look like a burger or it might look like tofu salad. But I hope not, with the tofu." He tipped his head. "Hand holding could be involved."

Alien possession? This boy had lost his mind.

He continued. "The hand holding is optional, but

it's nice I think. Underrated."

This was a puzzle that was not to be solved. I blew out a breath. It was time for an exit, but he was still blocking the door. "Don't you have a girlfriend?" I asked.

"No. That girl today? Just a girl I peer counsel. You have a boyfriend? The quiet one maybe?"

I didn't like that he knew about Mattie. "No," I said. "So?"

I paused. I didn't mean to pause. "I can't."

He stepped forward into the room. "I like you. You're not like other girls around here. They have two emotions: 'So much fun' and 'major drama.' You have a virtual, I don't know, rainbow of emotions without even talking. And I get this strange idea you might like me. I checked you out. My dad said you're a transplant here from Kellogg. Stepdad is an alumni. But if you want, I'm sure there's a way to make something work here?"

I blinked. The stirring in my stomach at his persistence was distracting me. I tried to focus. "Rainbow of emotions?"

He shrugged.

"You don't know me." I motioned a hand from my head down toward my shoes. "This is all an illusion." It was silly, but it was starting to make me feel sad.

His eyes narrowed like he was the one trying to figure out the riddle.

It was like explaining "three sheets to the wind" to those Haitian exchange students last year. Something was being lost in translation.

I waved my hand at him to move. "I have to go. I'm late for the park."

"Oh . . . I got it. You're a skater groupie."

My face was hot when I whipped back around. "You got a problem with skaters? Because FYI I'm actually the skater, not the groupie."

"Really?" He looked more disbelieving than repulsed or judgmental. But he still didn't seem to get that we might as well have been from different planets. He shrugged.

Maybe he was slow.

"Me being a skater girl isn't public knowledge, either, which is why this whole flirty thing won't work," I said. "It's not just because I'm a transplant. It's everything."

Cooper looked thoughtful for a second and rubbed his clean chin. "Skater girl, huh? That is very interesting." He was smiling again.

I crossed my arms. I wasn't sure if I should be more amused or irritated at his reaction. I bit back a smile. "Why is it interesting? You've been looking for lessons or . . . ?"

"Depends. What do you teach under the half pipe?"

"Ha. Nothing you need lessons on, obviously," I said, surprising myself.

He laughed. A good laugh.

I dropped my smile and moved around him into the hall. I walked past the kiln room toward the fire exits by the loading dock. We walked. Together.

I thought about my pact to not make any friends here, to be all business and use the opportunity to help get into college. A top college. To get something that was my own, and not just handed to me from my stepdad. I thought of the confrontation between Gav and Cooper's friends, and whatever all that was. I kept thinking all these thoughts, but as we reached the end of the hall he was still with me, and I wasn't trying all that hard to get rid of him.

When we got to the door I reached for the push bar, but his hand on my arm stilled me. He gave my sleeve a gentle tug until I faced him. Why did he have to smell so good?

I avoided his eyes but made no move to pull away. I wanted to stretch the moment, stay three inches from him, with his eyes on me, for as long as possible. But I also knew the next kiss would make it real.

He leaned closer, the three inches shrinking between us, but he still wouldn't close it. His eyes were searching mine. I hooked my arm around the back of his head and pulled him the rest of the way. I leaned back against the wall and we took our time finding the rhythm, though well aware of the time capsule we were in. When we broke away to breathe, he set his forehead against mine, which made the breathing thing even harder.

Reality stroked my stomach like a hot poker.

I slipped around him, my back already leaning against the push bar on the door. "This never happened either," I said.

"Wait. If you were to give me your number, could I text you and pretend I didn't?"

I smiled. He was catching on.

Chapter 5

Friday morning Cooper was getting to me, but not in a bad way. My phone was chirping as soon as I was out of the shower. Cooper texted me a smiley and the words: **Not sorry**. We texted back and forth while I dressed, and by the time I made it down for breakfast I was the one smiling like a freak.

I stepped into Landon's kitchen and paused. Mom was sitting next to Landon in the "nook" which was as big as the entire kitchen at our old house. They smiled at each other over soft boiled eggs, toast, and coffee. She looked good there. Natural. New hair, new clothes, new husband. Not to mention: new baby bump. It wasn't that I resented her getting what she wanted—a ticket out of the poverty my dad left us in when he took off, but it made me feel awkward how easy the transition was for her and not for me.

I was the same old me, but dressed up in a new uniform.

"Oh, good morning," my mom said, looking up.

I tucked away my phone in my pocket.

"Hey," I said. I gathered up cereal, bowl, milk, spoon, and perched at the counter with my back to them. To my left, Henry, my six-year-old brother, sat moving the crumbly remains of his usual gluten-free breakfast bar around with his fingers. With his dark hair and being dressed all in brown he was nearly blending right into the dark wood countertop. Even with the age difference, I had a sweet spot for the guy. Partly, I think, because he reminded me of Mattie. Mattie didn't have autism spectrum disorder like Henry, but for Henry, having ASD meant that he didn't talk a lot. He was also, among other things, "socially challenged." I could relate to that.

"Hey, dude," I said. He didn't answer, which he often didn't.

"Say 'hi,' Henry," Mom said.

Henry said "hi" without looking, and then started chanting a jaunty song in Spanish under his breath, which amused me.

"Do you want me to make you some eggs?" Mom asked as I poured the milk into my cereal.

I almost laughed. Eggs? Since when? "It's fine. I'm having cereal," I said, glancing back.

"It's no trouble," she said, even though everything about the way she stood up screamed effort: one hand pushing on the chair and the other supporting her pregnant belly.

I shoved a spoon full of granola and flakes into my mouth to stifle any back chat. This had to be for Landon's benefit, because Mom was never the make-you-eggs-for-breakfast kind of mom. At least not for me. My older brothers came four and six years before me and probably sucked all the mom energy from her. Henry was the last-ditch save-the-failing-marriage baby, which failed anyway. Besides, Henry was allergic to eggs, and just about every-thing else. Maybe she'd make eggs for the new baby.

I swallowed. "I'm cool," I said, giving them an enthu-siastic thumbs-up.

She and Landon both looked at me like I was some foreign object they'd never encountered before. Mom lowered herself back down. I started eating again, cursing myself that I'd forgotten my iPod or at least my math homework to pretend to look over. That sort of thing was usually good to discourage any chitchat.

I heard the bench seat in the nook creak. "Make sure she cleans her dishes," Landon said in a low voice. "She didn't clean them yesterday."

Mom must have nodded or smiled because I didn't hear her answer.

His dress shoes clicked on the linoleum until he was next to me. I looked up at him. He smiled. A pleasant,

41

yet practiced sort of smile that meant nothing. "Have a good day, Cassie." He patted my shoulder.

"Right," I said. "You too." But he was already walking away. He didn't even glance in Henry's direction. Just like Mattie: when you're quiet people seem to forget about you.

It wasn't like he was a bad guy. There wasn't anything I could find that was particularly sleazy or snobby or anything. Dude just wasn't really a kid person. He didn't hate us, not that I could tell anyway. He didn't know how to talk to us. Which was fine, I didn't know how to talk to him, either. Landon owned a car dealership, and in his spare time—other than hanging out seeing rom coms with Mom—he was into exactly two things: gluing together models of old ships in the garage and reading old paperback westerns. Seriously? Where would I even start?

Eventually, Mom shuffled out, too, reminding Henry to drink his juice and that he had to brush his teeth before school. I knew from experience he'd need another reminder or two. Henry's mind was on his crumbs again, or had never left them. The crumbs had become some kind of space soldiers by the sound of the laser guns he was imitating.

I tapped his shoulder. "Henry."

His head turned toward me, but his wide eyes stayed fixed somewhere over my left shoulder.

"Remember: people want to see your smile. That's how they know you like them. It makes them feel good, and then you feel good. Right?"

"Okay," he said.

I took my bowl to the sink and ran the water.

"Cass?"

I turned off the tap. "Yeah, bud?"

"Bye." His lips stretched into a forced wide smile.

×

At school I enjoyed the tension between Cooper and me. My eyes were magnetized to his body parts, whether he was coming or going in the hall. Unfortunately, I managed to score another detention with Sister Rita after completely zoning in class and answering her question with "I have no idea." Which burned me, because I knew everything there was to know about the Tuskegee experiment and damn syphilis. But I didn't think announcing that to the class would be doing myself any favors. I packed up my books and hid away from Cooper's distracting glances in the library over lunch. I studied up for my Civics exam and completed my French homework through the end of the week.

The afternoon had less dodging and more missing, as Cooper didn't revisit his locker for the last two classes.

I lingered in the art room at the end of the day, musing over the sunrise I'd added behind the boat. It tamed the murky waters, but felt cheesy.

Remembering my appointment with Sister Rita, I glanced around for a clock. I gave up looking among the tall shelves heaped with old art supplies and projects, and resorted to turning on my phone and checking it on the way to her classroom.

It chirped with a text from Cooper.

Peer CNSL, STDT CNSL. You?

I had made it to Sister Rita's class with less than a minute to spare.

Detentn, I sent back.

I moved my thumb to power down when it chirped again. I cursed the sound. I couldn't be late.

See u after?

The click of Sister's clogs were getting louder from inside the classroom. Mattie was coming to meet me, but there was no time to explain.

No

I hit SEND then powered off and slipped my phone away before it was finished with its tune.

Sister Rita held the door wide.

×

After detention, Mattie and I rounded the corner from the back of the school and onto the paved path that cut across the grass field. The path went through a patch of woods and opened up by the football stadium.

I normally avoided main paths, but figured with football practice over, there wouldn't be many people still coming and going. And it was a handy shortcut, popping us out within a block of the skate park.

But it was a dry, sunny day, so the grounds had more people hanging around than usual. A few straggling footballers were emerging from the woods on the path.

I tugged my hoodie down to my eyes and kept my chin low. We had our boards tucked close to our bodies. No riding until we were off school property. My rule, not the school's—though it could have been the school's, too. We practiced our ninja invisibility.

I was thinking about Cooper and the kisses, how crazy I was, and when I could get him to kiss me like that again when the voices ahead caused me to look up.

There he was. Cooper. He was with Devon and Eli, who were both dressed for football practice, standing on the grass next to the path just off the start of the woods. I watched as a runty freshman tried to scurry around them and tripped over one of the pointed tooth rocks that lined that path. His three-ring cracked down as he landed and the rings busted opened. The wind scooped up the freed papers and they began a random storm of white that soon spread the width of the field.

The tall one next to Cooper, Devon, laughed one of those laughs that was sure to get everyone's attention. Because something isn't funny to these guys until they can share it with everyone around. The laugh actually took on a pointing and clapping fest once the shorter one, the black kid, Eli, got into it with him.

I mean, really. Did guys like this have secret meetings on Public Humiliation 101 or was it just in their genes? People hanging around in the grass, or passing by on the path, joined in the expected laughing and staring.

There was movement next to me and I reached out to tug Mattie to a halt. There was no way I wanted to be caught in the middle of a scene. My eyes went to Cooper, who had already discovered me. We were locked in this little staring contest across the distance of about twenty feet, when Devon scooped up piles of paper and threw them up into the air. "It's snowing, Freshie!"

This had Eli doubled over.

I figured there had to be a saved-my-life-when-we-were-kids kind of story going on between Devon and Cooper. How else could you explain anyone enjoying the company of a sadist jock like Devon? Not five minutes in his vicinity and I was ready to make ugly with his face.

After the third "snowing, Freshie" outburst, Cooper finally stepped up. "Cool it, Devon. You're council president." His voice was low, like he'd grown tired of the game.

Eli snorted, then cleared his throat. "Yes, Devon. You should be setting an example," he said in a passable rendition of Headmaster Spanders's voice.

"Damn, Coop! Why you always breaking my balls?" Devon said to Cooper. There was an edge to his voice that surprised me.

Freshie was purple-faced as he stuffed the last of the papers in his bag. People were over the show and kept on with what they'd been doing before, so Mattie and I continued our way up the path.

Mattie hissed through his teeth as we approached the guys.

Cooper locked eyes with mine.

His ears were red, and without his smile, he looked thrown off his game. I wondered if it was my presence or his conscience that kept him from joining in the teasing.

I looked away without a smile or nod.

We had entered the canopy of trees and the sun was blocked out. Like day turning to twilight. One moment I was squinting my eyes, and the next they were adjusting to the dim.

"Hey!" a voice called behind us.

Mattie stopped to see who it was, so I had no choice but to stop and look, too.

Cooper's eyes searched mine as he approached, no doubt looking for a sign of warning or eagerness. I didn't give him either as I schooled the lines of my face into blankness. Breaking away from his friends to follow us wasn't exactly subtle.

The red from his ears had spread to the rest of his face like a fever, in a way that I might've found sexy if I wasn't determined not to. Besides, guys who don't take hints were useless.

He stopped a few feet from us, glancing at Mattie before speaking to me.

"Can we talk?" he said.

I rolled my eyes and turned away.

"I have a couple questions about my math homework. Heard you were good at . . . math."

Great. He was useless at lying, too. The pathetic urgency dripped from his words as his eyes pleaded. No one pleaded with pathetic urgency about math.

Despite the irritating behavior, having him this close had me fantasizing about his arms reaching around my waist, and I could almost feel my fingers combing up the back of his neck into his hair. I clamped down on the vision and reminded myself of Freshie. And that Mattie was watching us.

"I rock math, but you're a senior. I don't do precalc." I turned back down toward the path again, but was halted by Cooper's grip on my arm. Mattie stepped between us and gave Cooper a rough shove, dislodging Cooper's grasp on me.

What the fuck are you doing?

The swear-laced question coming from Mattie's head must have been loud enough for even Cooper to hear because he retreated a step.

He held up his hands. "I'm not looking for trouble." He looked around Mattie to me. "I suck." His eyes moved over my face. "I'm only in Geometry II."

He even went so far as to dig around his bag and pull out his book. He sat down on the bench and found a notebook and a pen. I had to work to stifle a smile. Ridiculous.

Mattie was rolling his eyes. I couldn't blame him. It was time to give Mister Clueless a clue. I tugged on Mattie's sleeve until I had his attention, but avoided eye contact. "Bug off, okay? I'll catch you guys up at the park. Ten minutes."

Mattie shook his head. *Why? You saw what they did!*

What could I say? I didn't know why. "Just do it, please?"

Cooper and I were silent as Mattie slapped down his board and rode off. The whir of his wheels quieted to nothing. There was no sign of any more ballers on the path. Still, Cooper looked back and forth before packing away his book and zipping up his bag. He stepped over the jaggy-teeth rocks and into the trees. I watched him stop several feet inside the lip of thick trees and set down his backpack. It wasn't far enough in where I had to wonder if he could get away with raping me and chopping me into bite-size pieces, but far enough to give our voice a muffle and a bit of cover against someone coming down the path. I didn't really think Cooper was the raping or chopping or eating-human-flesh kind of guy, but he was confusing the crap out of me so far.

I made my way through the tangled trees to where he stood.

He wasn't smiling. "Go ahead. Say it."

"Fine," I said. "This—whatever this is—isn't going to work. I despise your friends. Typical St. B snobs."

He leaned in. "My friends?"

"You didn't even help that Freshie kid!" I threw a pointed arm back toward the incident.

"Did you help him?"

The question threw me off. "What?"

"Blakely. The 'Freshie'? Did you guys help him? You know—pick up his papers?" He made a vague motion with his hand.

I let my bag slide off my shoulder onto the ground. "No. But that's not the same."

"Why? He's not your friend? It didn't cross your take-action line?"

I hated it, but I thought about what he was saying. "Something like that. So? I wasn't the one harassing him."

"Neither was I. You know, Blakely goes to this school, too. Is he another St. B snob? And he's not a Freshie. He's a sophomore. Isn't that what you are? You probably have him in some of your classes and you didn't even know his name."

I thought hard about the mousy brown-haired kid. I couldn't pull him into a memory of any of my classes. But that didn't mean it wasn't true. Which I guess was his point.

"I'm not here to make friends. I have my own friends,"
I said.

"Do your friends ever do or say things that are embarrassing or piss you off? Or are Frogtown boys perfect
like you?"

I didn't like where he was going with this. Of
course there were times that Gav shot off his mouth to
a younger skater or Franklin hollered out to girls in a
way that would earn him a punch in the chest from me.
Then there was the way we all talked about the richies
at St. B's. Like they were all the same.

Cooper broke into my thoughts. "I don't like my
friends all the time, but they're my friends, you know?
Sometimes I laugh at the stuff they pull, but I also
peer counsel a half-dozen kids just like Blakely. I don't
think you could give me the names of six kids in your
entire grade."

I opened my mouth, just to close it again. Six? I'd
be hard pressed to give him the names of three.

"So, who's the snob, Cass?" he asked, his voice dropping when he said my name.

"Me?"

Cooper sighed. "You're not. That's just a made up word
anyway. Assholes, snobs, richies, losers, nerds . . . gutter
punks? This doesn't have to be the fucking Breakfast
Club." He stepped closer. "I think you're . . . interesting. I
don't care who you hang with or who you don't hang with.

I want to get to know you. I want to know why you're here—even though you hate us and already want a reason to push me away, even though there's a pull in your eyes when I get close."

The absence of horny hunger in his eyes was making it impossible to box him in with any male creature I had ever tangled with outside my group of friends. He stood there looking at me, really looking at me. It terrified me. He was looking right into me like no one else ever had.

I swallowed before taking a step closer. "Just me and you. Figuring things out. No one else knows, okay?"

He smiled and I figured Mattie might have to put up with me being late. Again.

Chapter 6

I spent all weekend with Mattie, Gav, and Franklin. My guys. Saturday we hit the big skating park by Lake Harriet in the a.m. and ended the afternoon by soaking up the rays and the sudden warm-up, throwing our leftover sandwich bits at the geese and trying to get them to chase Franklin. On Sunday we scraped up some cash and went to an afternoon Steve Buscemi marathon at Oak Street Cinema. So it didn't raise any eyebrows when I begged off boarding after school Monday to catch up on homework. It was true, I had a ton, but that's not what I was doing.

Cooper led me by the hand into the woods behind the school. We'd arrived separately, of course, meeting just off the lip of the path. We made our way deeper into the woods, then sat on a fallen tree. He told me about Eli being showed up in gym class during weight lifting by the captain of the girls' basketball team. I laughed at his imitation of Eli's pouting face. I told him about Franklin's own pouting over the weekend when he went over-the-top celebrating his stuck single spin, only to be showed up by a younger kid doing a double. Cooper laughed.

His phone played a tune and he glanced at the screen before turning it off. "Devon." His lips twitched. "I wish I could quit that guy."

I laughed. "I wish you could, too."

Cooper looked around and found a hollow spot from a rotted-out knot. He stuck his phone inside. "Out of sight . . ."

The laughter died down and we took advantage of our aloneness. His kisses were sweet and soft. Not rushed or insistent. We took a breath and I glanced at my watch.

"You have to go?" he said.

"This is lame, but I have homework. I don't want to fall behind."

"Yeah, yeah. Me too."

"You could . . . come over? To study?" I asked.

He smiled. "Would that be weird?"

It was totally weird, thinking about him in my room. But I shrugged. "Let's find out."

×

We sat cross-legged on my floor. Our knees touching and homework spread around us. If it wasn't my own house, I might have been looking to bail. Somehow we went from touring my room, to making out on my bed, to me fielding an awkward phone call from my mom. Then, after settling on the floor together with our books, Cooper's back stiffened and he seemed to have something more serious than homework on his mind.

"Let's play a game."

"What kind of game?" I asked carefully, thinking that maybe I'd read his mood all wrong.

"Like Forty Questions? I'll ask you a personal question, like 'What's your favorite color?' and then you can ask me one."

I got that people had these conversations. I got that most couples had a need to discover each other's favorites, share one's dreams, and hold each other's secrets. But I wasn't even sure if what we were was a "couple," and if we were, all of that wasn't me. I wasn't built to freely give away parts of myself to someone else, no matter how good they are at kissing.

I hummed a response that wasn't really a yes or a no. He was watching me and I stayed very still. Finally, I said, "I don't really like games like that."

He waited me out. So I just waited. I could tell by the tense slope of Cooper's shoulders he was frustrated.

"I feel frustrated," he said. "I want to get to know you, but I can feel your walls going up."

I gave him a nod of acknowledgment, which was all I was willing to give. I mean, I wanted to, but I couldn't stop the doors slamming around what was mine.

"Okay," he said. "I'll start. I'll share something I haven't really shared with many people." He pressed his pointer finger into my knee. "I don't expect anything in return, I just want you to have that piece of me."

I closed my eyes and waited, resisting the urge to stop him.

He took a deep breath. "Two years ago my mom was diagnosed with breast cancer and I thought she was going to die."

The words lit a fire in my chest and my eyes snapped open to meet his.

He continued. "Instead of bringing us closer, I found it easier to pull back. Or, I just thought it would be easier when she died, if we weren't so close."

"What happened?"

"Well, she lived. But I don't think that distance ever went away."

I nodded in encouragement, but he didn't say any more. I realized he was waiting for me. And suddenly, I wanted to give him something, too. I opened my mouth and let the words fall out before I could think better of it. "I told my mom, the day Mattie went in for his cancer surgery, that if he died I would need to walk him to heaven in case he got lost. I sat in my closet all day with a suitcase packed in case we had to go."

"A suitcase for heaven? What did you pack?" His fingertips traced circles on both of my knees.

"Blankets and sandwiches."

"Very practical."

"Well, I was seven."

He leaned back, resting his weight on his hands behind him. "Do you ever feel like you're still waiting?"

"What do you mean?"

"Sometimes I feel like I'm bracing myself, that even though she's in remission, she's still going to die."

"We all die eventually." I meant to crack the tension, but his eyes squinted in determination.

"Yeah. But I think that's why I still pull away. Does that ever happen to you?"

I'm not stupid, and neither is Cooper. I could tell by the way he was looking at me that this wasn't just about Mattie's cancer.

"Mattie didn't die. But my dad left, and sometimes I think that not only do we all die, and life is temporary and all that shit, but so is love." As soon as it was out I felt the flash of fear. I felt exposed, like I'd just tipped the balance and shared too much.

"What—?"

"My favorite color is green," I said suddenly. So I could breathe again. So I felt safe.

×

A week later, Cooper and I were in the art hallway again after school. A warm alternative to the woods when it rained. I was working hard at offering pieces of myself, in return for the pieces that Cooper kept offering me. But the kissing part came easier.

Cooper mumbled into the crook of my neck. "Text Mattie."

"He's probably already out there waiting," I said.

All last week I'd given Mattie and the guys excuses. Excuses that would give me more time with Cooper. Now all the guys were bugging me about bailing on them all week for "homework" and "detention" and crap lies like that.

Sunny and warmish for another four days, and I'd made it to the park once. In September in Minnesota, warm and sunny was fleeting and in a blink could be taken over by twenty-degree temperature drops. And so it was today. With rain.

"That's why you should text him"—he paused to kiss my neck again, which was driving me mad—"so he can stop waiting for you."

"What should I say? Besides clueing him in to the fact that it's raining. In case he hasn't noticed."

He kissed his way up to my jaw before answering. "Clubs. You need to join some school clubs to beef up your apps for college."

My eyes snapped open. "I do?"

Cooper came up to look at me. "Haven't you been meeting with your guidance counselor?"

"That guy is a total creeper. I've been avoiding him. I swear he's probably bumped uglies with at least five girls in my grade alone."

"Really?" He made a face, then shook off the thought. "Not to worry. The president of the peer counselor club can meet with you"—he checked his watch—"right now."

"How awesomely convenient for me," I said.

He leaned in for a kiss but I held him back. "I really should go talk to Mattie. Five minutes, okay?" I hated that it was a question. I was always the one to set limits with boys. I was always in control. But I could see from his face that we were making the decision together. I nodded along with him.

A shock of fear flashed in my chest and I tightened my hold on him. I liked him. A lot. The more I went down this road the more painful the crash and burn would be. This one's gonna hurt when he leaves.

"Meet me by my car?" he asked, peeling my arms from around him.

"No."

His eyebrows pinched in confusion.

"I mean, I'll meet you somewhere, but no way I'm getting into a car with you in the school parking lot. Way too public."

He sighed. "Meet me at my house. Is there a bus that can get you to Summit and Hamline Ave.?"

"6C. Every eleven minutes," I answered automatically.

He pulled out a notebook and jotted down his address. Summit Avenue. The boy lived on Summit. The freaking governor lived on Summit. I folded it and shoved it in the pocket of my school hoodie.

"Come to the back door. The key is on top of the doorframe," he said, before dropping one more kiss on my cheek. I resisted the urge to reach out and grab him. Hold on to him. Never let him go.

"What's wrong?" he said.

"I was thinking about how much it's going to suck when it's over." I shook my head. I shouldn't have said that out loud. This guy was frying my brain like smack.

"We just started this. I'm not going anywhere."

"You always have to plan for good-bye."

"I don't like to say good-byes."

"Nobody likes good-byes. But it's better to say it than just leave. Then everybody knows you are going." I had the presence of mind to close my mouth. I was saying too much.

He looked me over. "Are you talking about your dad?"

I chastised myself. This conversation wasn't happening. I had to shut it down. "No," I said. "I'm not talking about anything."

×

I pulled my hoodie forward as I pushed through the door and stepped over to the shelter of the loading dock. I didn't see Mattie perched in his usual spot under the covered loading dock, which would have been dry, or pulling ollies in the rain. I started to figure he must have bailed, when I saw a familiar fluorescent green at the corner of the building. We gave Gav all kinds of crap when he got that jacket at the thrift, but he insisted it was his "signature color" (whatever that meant), and that he'd never get hit by a car wearing it. And he hasn't. But nobody we knew had ever been hit by a car.

I was about to call out to him, but when he shifted his weight away from the wall I saw that he was talking to some tall kid. Shaved head, long nose, complicated teeth. I sheltered my eyes from the insistent drizzle. Coming down the stairs to get a better look, I didn't notice the water-filled pothole until my size nine sank in two inches deep.

"Shit!" slipped out of my mouth, causing them both to turn. The guy with the shaved head rounded the corner and was gone.

Gav watched him go, then jogged over to me carrying his board. "You turn your phone on ever? I thought you'd been hit by a car." He jerked his head to get his bangs out of his face. His hair was so black when it was wet that it looked like ink, except for the piece of green. He bounced on the balls of his feet and flashed his sideways smile that always made him look like he was up to something.

"For real? Come on Gav, I've been out of class for ten minutes," I said.

"And Mattie sent you a text ten minutes ago. We're bailing to my house."

"Yeah." I hesitated. "I'm gonna . . . take a rain check."

Gav let out a hiss. "Big surprise. Making new friends, Cass?"

"Are you?"

He blew out a laugh. "St. B snobs? Naw. Guy was just trying to bum a smoke from me. From me! That richie should be buying me a smoke." He stopped bouncing. "I know your mom has forgotten where she comes from, but you won't, right?"

That one hurt. "It's just the precollege stuff. It's just today."

"It's not just today. You were getting gone before the first day at this school."

"What? That's bullshit."

"Is it? When's the last time you talked to me about real shit?" he said before I could answer—not that I had an answer. "Before your dad left. Then after you just shut it down and shut us out."

"You're wrong, drama queen. I just have to join these clubs. That's right now, that's today. Skating half pipes and playing video games isn't going to get me into college."

I hated lying, but he had my back up. I did need to get into college. Shouldn't he be more supportive?

"Well, you have fun with that. One step closer to leaving us for good, huh?"

"I'm not leaving you. I'd never leave you guys. I only left the neighborhood."

"Keep telling yourself that."

×

Sitting on the bus I thought about what Gav said. The lying-induced guilt was gnawing at me. But then I thought *screw him* because I was at St. B's for a reason. Everyone knew I was going to college. We all said we never wanted to stay in the neighborhood forever. Never wanted to live the stereotypes and be what people expected of us coming from where we did. Which was nothing except a rap sheet and an early explosion of the next generation of welfare brats.

It was still raining, more like a sheet than a drizzle, by the time the bus landed me two houses down from Cooper's.

Summit Avenue was a string of some of the oldest houses in St. Paul—and the nicest. I passed the governor's mansion on the way and almost bailed. I could handle that Cooper had money, but his parents better not have servants. Or be into politics. Or be lawyers.

I checked myself. It was about Cooper. Me and Cooper. I had to put a stop to that snobby crap.

I came around through the alley and approached the back door like he told me. I reached for the top of the doorframe, but the door opened before my fingers even found the spare key. Cooper pulled me off balance toward him. He swept a kiss on my nose.

"Hi. Let's get you out of these wet things."

I pushed him back into the kitchen and found my feet. "Right. You wish."

He wagged his eyebrows at me. I turned my head so he wouldn't catch my smiling-like-an-idiot face and looked around the room. The kitchen was newer than ours, and larger for sure, but not scary nice. Someone had stenciled white ducks in yellow bows above the cupboards. It was country themed. Not exactly the straight-from-a-magazine chic I'd been expecting.

The ducky theme continued below the cupboards, too. Salt and pepper shakers—and was that a cookie jar?—sat on the counter.

"Quack," I said with a smile.

"Yeah, I know. It's like, her thing. She even has a curio cabinet full of figurines and a stuffed one on her bed."

"That's . . . creepy."

"She's out of control."

"No, I mean you, using the words 'curio cabinet' and 'figurines.' Ruins every fantasy I've ever had about you."

I enjoyed his speechless blinking.

"If I promise not to use those words again can I be . . . invited back to your fantasies?" he asked.

"Maybe. But, so you know, 'wicker' and 'crochet' are absolute deal breakers."

He smiled. "I'll watch myself."

There was a main floor laundry room off the kitchen, with the stairs going up in between the two rooms. I followed him up to a hallway that had a picture-lined wall on one side, and a railing on the other that opened up to a view of the living room below. I put my hands on the railing to stave off that vertigo feeling and looked down.

Cooper pulled me down the hall to his bedroom.

I'm not sure what I was expecting, but his room was a mess. Serious shit-crap everywhere. No moldy food or gerbils making nests, but books, discs, clothes, receipts . . . stuff lay wherever it fell. For some reason this made me happy.

Cooper looked around with me. "As you can see I had enough time to pick up while I waited."

"Thanks."

He swept the books and clothes off his bed and onto the floor in one swoop.

"Are you thinking what I'm thinking?" he asked.

I glanced down at the bed and my mouth went dry. I'm not a baby in the experience department. When you're constantly surrounded by guys, things happened. Forgettable things. But with those guys I never found it hard to control them or myself. But with Cooper . . .

"Um—"

"Chips and pop. I'll be right back."

He left the room, shutting the door behind him. I exhaled, blowing out my stupidity. I used the time to change into what was supposed to be my boarding outfit for the afternoon. Once done (sixty seconds flat) I tied my hair up into its "afterschool" knot.

I sat down on his bed and looked around. The mess was sort of comforting. Along with that cheesy duck-themed kitchen, this disorder was endearing. Like not everything in his life was as perfect and orderly and cool as I'd imagined. I guess the messy part of him was the part that was attracted to me.

When he came back in, he tossed the chip bag down next to me and handed me a Coke. His eyes moved over me.

"Geotrash?" he asked, bringing attention to my shirt. He said it with a chuckle. Like how obvious I would like that kind of emo-pop-punk band.

I covered my shirt with crossed arms. I suddenly felt all too transparent.

He took in my silence with some of his own. He

stepped away with a half turn toward his closet, his fingers already unfastening the buttons on his shirt.

"Don't."

He turned back toward me. "I'm just gonna change my shirt."

"Don't," I said with an edge I didn't think I meant. Or maybe I did.

"Don't what?" he asked.

"Change." I turned away. This was a bad idea. This whole thing was shit.

I didn't hear him approach over the noise in my head, but felt him tugging on my arm. He kept on tugging until I was sitting down next to him on the bed. He set his hand behind me, leaning close. "What's wrong?"

"Nothing."

"Seriously."

I took a deep breath. "I don't fit with you. Whatever preppy or sporty or precious, rich hipster shit you change into is not going to fit with me. Any way you look at it, it's like the—the square peg in the round hole or round peg in the square hole."

He grabbed on to my hands, which had become fists. "We already do fit, in all the ways that matter."

I shook my head. I wasn't going to let his arguments tip my train of thought. "Up until now, in our uniforms, I can pretend we're the same. But like this? As me? It's harder to pretend."

"I don't want you to pretend with me."

"I know. But this all just reminds me that I need— need to keep this simple."

He chewed on my words along with his lip. "What do you mean simple? Hiding out isn't simple."

"But it's not complicated. Trying to make this something it's not makes it feel complicated," I said.

"Well, what do you want it to be? Like if we lived on the moon and nobody knew us?"

"We don't live on the moon. But St. Bernadette's might as well be compared to the high school I came from."

Cooper moved closer to me on the bed. "What do you want, Cass?"

"I want . . . I want . . ." But I didn't know what I wanted. Or I couldn't find the words to compact the million feelings I was having and smash them into a couple of sentences. Besides the way his eyebrows took on that pained look and the way he rubbed the pad of his thumb against his lower lip. He leaned closer as he waited for me to formulate a sentence, which distracted me even more.

So I tugged the collar of his uniform shirt and kissed him like trying to itch a scratch or scratch an itch that won't be satisfied. I wanted him closer and deeper. To overtake my senses and block out all the thoughts that threatened to ruin whatever this was.

I flopped back on the bed and pulled him with me. Cooper broke off the kiss. "Hey, hey. Slow down." He smoothed some stray damp hairs back from my forehead, and I had to brace against the spin. His kisses could set my head spinning faster than those once-in-a-blue-moon pulls I take on Gav's sister's cigarettes.

And could he be more perfect? What guy tells a girl to slow down?

"What's so funny?" he asked.

"Nothing. I don't know. You've managed to kiss me stupid."

He smiled and then his arms were around me and it took me a sec to actually figure out that he was hugging me. Just hugging me. Something welled up inside me so fast that shit if it didn't scare me half to death. I closed my eyes in his room, in his house, and set my chin against his shoulder.

"I just want you," he whispered into my hair, as if thinking aloud. For all I knew he had been, because he tightened his grip like he was afraid of what he'd just said. Or was that me that tightened?

I opened my eyes and spotted a crazy-looking red camera on his bedside table. I crawled over and grabbed it up with one hand. Curling back into him I held the camera above. I looked up but his face was still nuzzled into my neck when the flash took.

I let him go with a squeal of surprise as the camera whirred to life and printed a credit card–size pic out of the top. Cooper laughed but kept his arms around me as I wiggled loose enough to check the camera out more closely.

"It's instant. My grandma got it for me," he said.

"It's fucking sweet is what it is."

We both sort of exhaled as we stared at the picture.

"Here's me," I said, and tossed the picture down on the bed.

Chapter 7

I arranged and rearranged my book bag for the fourth time as I stood in front of my locker, knowing if someone was watching, I looked seriously OCD. But no one ever did notice me. I stole another glance down the hall as it thinned out.

I hated that Cooper was late, but even more, that with only two weeks into this . . . whatever . . . he had me anticipating him. I smelled him a second before he slipped around me to his locker.

"Who are you waiting for?" he said to his lock with a smile.

"Prince Charming, but he's made me late, so I think I'll tell him to bite it," I said in a low voice.

He glanced at me, his brow worrying into a furrow.

His lock clicked open. "It's Thursday. You said you're skating today, right?"

"Yeah, I know, just felt like . . . waiting. No biggie." I crouched down to pull out one more book, annoyed at my own embarrassment. My hand froze as his finger twisted into my leather bracelet, his shoulder touching mine.

I shot a look around. Black Glasses (Brett?) glanced down at us and away. No one else was around.

"It's nice. Where'd you get it? Is that your initials on the charm?" Cooper asked.

He knew darn well where I'd gotten it and what it said. I'd told him Mattie gave it to me. "Are you on crack snacks? What are you doing?" I whispered without looking at him, like maybe if I didn't move he'd stop touching me.

He tugged on the bracelet. "Would it be so wrong for you to look at me? Talk to me? With other people around?"

"You can talk, just don't touch." I wrenched my hand back, but the twist of his finger and the slack on the band caused it to slip right off. I reached back for it just as Devon the Wonder Jerk stepped up. I did a quickie glance up at him, and saw that he was scrolling through his phone, then glanced at us. When I looked back at Cooper, the hand that had held my bracelet was in his pocket, and he was holding out a pencil with his other hand.

"Thanks," I said, taking it. I stood up and started going through the junk on the top shelf of my locker. I'd have to wait for Devon to bug off to get my bracelet back.

"Where 's Eli?" Cooper asked.

"Outside, picking on the uglies." He punched a few buttons on his phone. "Let's do this," Devon said.

Cooper blew out a loud sigh. "I don't know if—"

"This was your idea," Devon said.

"I know."

"What are you looking at?" Devon said to me, and I realized I was staring.

I shook my head and looked away as Cooper slammed his locker. "Let's go."

Then there was a whir of dark hair, a lot of it, as someone launched into Cooper's arms. After what seemed rather excessive for any normal greeting, he set her down on her feet, though her hands like tentacles kept their latch on his arms. The brunette girlie again. Really? Is this how we greet our peer counselors?

A dark bruise wrapped around her wrist where her sleeve had slipped back, like she'd slept in her watch. It was the only flaw I could see, and I was really looking for them. She was some kind of cultural mix that made her skin a perfect honey brown, and her body had curves in just the right places.

"Marilyn—" Cooper started, but she interrupted.

"You guys don't have to do this," she said, but I

could see that she was smiling with her full lips. Beaming, really.

Cooper started to move, Devon already making paces up the steps toward the front door, but the girl was dragging her feet, a hand still glued to his sleeve. "This means so much to me," she said.

Cooper cleared his throat. "This ends today. He's not going to know what hit him."

"I won't tell anyone." Her voice got real low, but she glanced around like she would love people to be noticing them. "What's between us is just between us, right?"

Then, swear to God, she tippytoed right up and kissed my man on his cheek.

Devon was yelling at Cooper to hurry up from the top of the stairs. "Come on. We have an ass that needs kicking."

No way. I was in a shock-like trance. I watched with the sick fascination of a drive-by disaster. I stared all the mental heat I could right into Cooper's back, willing him to turn around and face me. A locker slamming across from me broke my trance. As Cooper disappeared through the doors I contemplated the possible duality of his personality. Could he be the Jekyll and Hyde of Saint Bernadette's?

I glanced at my watch. Late.

How could he touch me like that, talk to me like that, and then go off hugging that brown-haired thing and run off to beat up some kid?

A horn blaring in my left ear was the first sign that I was zoning. The second was Mattie's mom-arm slamming into my chest. The sudden stop had me back on my ass and my board sailed through the intersection without me. I saw it bounce against the opposite curb before the white Prius turned in front of us, driver giving us the finger for good measure. Mattie shook his head, pointing at the light.

We stop on red, remember?

"I know. Just zoning," I said as I hopped back to my feet.

He blew out a sigh like my whole distraction was an annoyance to him. The light changed and Mattie dropped onto his board. He smacked his fist into his hand at some kids who were getting all touchy with my board across the street.

I needed to focus on my riding to avoid being road cheese. I tucked it all away and did a couple lazy esses and watched as Mattie did a rail grind on a bus bench.

We approached the park from the baseball field side. I lifted my chin and scanned ahead. There, where the grass met the concrete of the skate park, I spotted three St. Bernadette uniforms. They were squared off against— oh, shit—Gav and his bright green accessories.

Whatever was going down, it didn't look pretty. I could hear the angry tones and see the pointed fingers even from a hundred feet out. Then one of them turned his head just enough and I nearly fell off my board. It was Cooper. Of course it was.

For worlds colliding, this was the worst possible scenario.

Behind Gav, Franklin was closing in, making his way swiftly from the half pipe. Devon, tall next to Cooper, started shoving. I was still five feet out, but I bailed on my board and started to run through the grass.

I didn't really have a plan other than to get in between them to break up the testosteroni thing they had going on. I reached out as Gav pushed who I could now see was Eli, but in midlunge I caught what must have been Devon's sucker punch on the back of my left shoulder. I heard someone yell "fuckers." I think it was Franklin, as he flew at Devon and I was knocked down. Something that felt like an anvil, but was more likely someone's knee banging into my head. As I tried to get up, I was stepped on more than once. I covered my spinning head until someone scooped me up and dragged me free from swinging limbs. I opened my eyes and saw that it wasn't Mattie, but Cooper.

I recoiled from the blood that was dripping from his nose and all over his sweatshirt, and when he held me tight I squirmed and started slamming my fists into his chest. "You asshole!"

Before he could defend himself a shadow covered us.

My achy head lolled a bit to see Gav, holding his board like a bat, his eyes zeroed in on Cooper.

"You let her go," Gav said.

I could hear the other guys shuffling around us.

"Hey, man—" someone said.

"Shut up!" someone else yelled back.

Gav kept his eyes trained on Cooper. "Don't look at her. Look at me or there'll be a whole lot more blood coming outta that head of yours."

Cooper eased his grip on me and I sank back to my knees. A siren chirped from the baseball diamond side of the park. There was more movement around us, but Cooper, Gav, and I were locked in our own frozen staring contest. Mattie stepped in front of Gav. He pulled on my elbow until I found my feet.

You okay?

I nodded.

It wasn't until Devon called his name twice that Cooper rose from his squat. Another stream of blood fell from his nose, and he blocked it with the back of his hand.

The ringing in my ears was the only sound. Like the rest of the world was standing still with us.

Mattie pushed my board against my chest until my hands figured out how to hold it. When he stepped away I saw Gav was already riding the path and Franklin was two board-lengths ahead of him.

I was still in slow motion as I turned to see Devon and Eli pulling Cooper along, wiping his nose on his sleeve and glancing back in my direction. A St. Paul police squad was parked at the curb. The red-haired cop rolled his window down as the guys came through the fence opening. Devon yelled out something to the cop who tipped his head back to laugh.

I winced as pain shot through my scalp and I jerked my head. Mattie was holding up his fingers.

You're bleeding.

"Yeah, well, thanks to you guys starting a rumble on my head," I said.

He jutted out his chin across the field. *You know those other guys?*

I took a minute to breathe because it felt like I hadn't in a while. Cooper was walking away. "No. I don't know them at all."

But the blond. He's the one—

"Shut up, Mattie."

He pulled me along by the hand down the path that led around the picnic area and to the kiddie park. There was no way the cops were going to throw up any road blocks over a fight in the park, no matter who the boys' daddies were. But Mattie knew I needed time to regroup before meeting up with Gav and Franklin.

We crawled under the climbing structure as kids thumped along over our heads. I sat down in the cool sand and folded my legs crisscross. I held my board on my knees. I closed my eyes and felt Mattie settle in next to me. He peeled off his sweatshirt and tossed it to me. I held it to my head to staunch the bleeding. I closed my eyes. Mattie kept the silence. He knew to keep his mouth shut and let me think.

Chapter 8

I'm not proud to say it, but I was hiding. I'd managed to get through the entire morning without going to my locker, and therefore had managed to avoid Cooper. He'd texted me four times since yesterday, and I left them unanswered. It's not that I wasn't sure. If jumping one of your friends isn't a deal breaker, I don't know what is. Besides, a two-week relationship or whatever this was, was nothing to get all choked up about. That's . . . what I kept telling myself.

I wasn't afraid of him. But I was afraid I'd lose it and end up being expelled for getting into a boxing match with him in the middle of the hall. Between the fight and whatever was going on with Marilyn made me want to break his nose. But that wasn't what mattered.

Gav. Gav was my friend and this thing with Cooper had to end. Period. I wasn't here to make friends, and there was no room for an exception.

After Civics I swung back to my locker and he was waiting. He looked pathetic with his forehead against the door. I bolstered by telling myself it wasn't emotional. I zenned down the anger, banished the pain, and got ready for business.

I dialed my combo without glancing at him. We both busied ourselves with nothing until the late bell for fifth period rang and the hall emptied out. I turned, not full facing him, but giving him about forty-five degrees.

"Are you okay?" he asked before I could start my prepared speech.

I pulled my head back as he reached his fingertips toward the Band-Aid on my forehead. "I need my bracelet back," I said.

He started to reach again, this time for my arm. "Cass—"

I smacked his hand away. "Don't."

I did a quick look around to make sure no one nearby was getting an earful. "I don't want to fight about it. This whole thing was stupid. I should've known that someone like you would—"

"Someone like me?" He barely managed to keep his voice low. I'd actually gotten a rise out of him. "You know, you get all high and mighty over how everyone is such an asshole—so judgmental and all that crap—

but look at you. Are you even going to give me a chance to explain?"

I squared off and let the anger come back up. "Oh, so there's a perfectly good reason why you jumped one of my best friends who you've never even met?"

"I didn't know he was your friend. And we did not jump him."

"Oh? 'We have an ass that needs kicking?'"

He dropped his eyes and looked around like the answer might be written on the floor between us.

I rolled my eyes. "I just need my bracelet back."

He shook his head. "No."

"No? You don't get a souvenir."

"I don't want a souvenir. I want you to hear me out," he said.

I banged my locker shut and started to walk away. Cooper clamped my elbow and steered me around the corner to a dead end hallway by the janitor's closet.

"Don't do this," he said.

I pulled my arm away and jammed my fists into his chest. "You did this!" I hated how shrieky my voice was getting.

"I had a reason. Your friend, Gav, is a dealer," he said.

I pulled back and crossed my arms. I huffed out half a breath to get my mind around what he'd just said. "That's bullshit."

"It's true. I don't usually make it my business, but when he's pushing on freshmen—"

"Pushing? Who said that?"

"Marilyn, that girl I peer counsel? She tells me things; trusts me. She said he bullied her into it. There were tears. What was I supposed to do?"

"Well, maybe she had a reason to lie."

"Why would she lie?" He paused, then shook his head. "There's no way she was lying."

"Come on, Cooper, a freshman gets to bend your ear, play the victim card?"

"It is not like that. She's just a sweet girl," he said.

"*And* she's sweet? A good girl, too, I bet. Are her parents alumni like yours? Maybe you guys can go public?"

Cooper stood up straight; his cheeks were red. He backed me against the wall with his stare, and his arms stretched on either side of me.

"I was never the one who wanted to keep this a secret. That has always been you. Besides, what do you care? You're breaking up with me, right?"

The smell of him was confusing me, and so was his closeness. I had to lower my eyes to speak.

"Yes, I am," I said, and made a point to raise my chin. I wasn't going to let him bully me. Let the sweet girl have him and all his lies. But the nerve endings in my arms were starting a wild protest. I tightened my hold on them to stop the shaking.

He stepped away and I had to fight the impulse to grab the front of his shirt. "Thanks for hearing me out, Cass. I really appreciate you trusting me enough to give me the benefit . . ." He shook his head and let the rest of the sentence fall off when his voice caught. He cleared his throat. "But who am I? Just one of the snobs, right?"

×

Art class finished out my day. I spent the whole period adding on layers and layers of color. The sunrise had turned stormy again. I dabbed and brushed my way through the whole class only thinking of Cooper and cursing myself for letting him hurt me this much. When the bell rang I texted Mattie that I didn't feel up to the park. He texted back that it looked like rain anyway, and to come over later for movies.

I mixed the Creole green into the jay blue with a dab of white and swirled. But the beauty of my creation soon swirled into a pile of puce crap.

Shit all.

I dropped the paint palate onto the stool next to me. I stared at the painting, which had somehow become sad and moody. I hated it.

Cooper was right; it was me pushing the secrecy thing. There was no way Mattie would understand how I could be with a guy who jumped Gav, even if it came out he was dealing.

Oh, Gav. What are you doing?

I heard the squeak next to me of the metal stool scraping the concrete floor. I knew without looking it was Cooper. He lifted the paint tray and set it on the next stool before sitting down. He yanked my stool closer to him, between his knees.

He reached out and took my hand, making our clasped hands fall against his leg. And I let him.

We didn't talk at first, but after a minute of looking at his drooping red face and moist eyes, I gave up any pretense and leaned my head against his chest. He ran a hand up into the back of my hair.

"I'm sorry," I said into his collared shirt, inhaling his scent one last time.

He blew out all his breath and I felt his Adam's apple bob as he spoke. "It's fine. I know how bad it looked."

I pulled back. "No. I'm sorry. Because this isn't going to work."

He let go of his grip on my hand and wiggled his fingers from the hold they had on mine. He looked at me until I looked away. He knew. He had to know this couldn't possibly work.

I watched him walk away, like some kind of surreal reality. I sat there. I stared at mountains of green and blues, wanting to crawl right in and never go home.

Then the panic hit my chest like a jolt and I was on my feet. I grabbed up my bag and ran to the back door. I pushed through and met the rain face first as

I hustled down the loading dock steps. I rounded the building and scanned the parking lot on the north side. A few cars remained, but I didn't even know which one was Cooper's. Back out front I checked the intersection where the freezing rain was turning into a fine layer of slush. Friday meant most people were in a hurry to leave, and no one was lingering around in the rain. I couldn't spot a single uniform.

I pulled out my phone.

My hands shook with a violent shiver as I wiped my thumb over the wet screen.

What would I say? This time I knew I had done it. It was me who left him.

I heard footfalls splashing behind me. Spinning around, I saw him. Cooper. With his bag slung over and his head down, shielding himself from the rain coming down the front steps of the school. Without letting doubt creep in anymore, I spanned the distance in leaps and jumped right into him when he was still coming down. He didn't see me. I toppled him over and he landed on his butt, but he was smiling.

"I'm sorry I'm sorry I'm sorry," I said in between the kisses I was painting all over his face.

He got his hands up to my face and directed my lips to his. We said everything that needed to be said, that couldn't be with words, in the sweetest way possible. We would try. All we could do was try.

We settled into a hug as the puddle of rain on the step was probably seeping into Cooper's pants. He didn't complain. I was kind of glad we were hunkered down like that, in between the walls that lined either side of the stairs. No one to see. But as I looked up I could have sworn I saw a face and a figure through the glass on the left side of the door. They were gone. Either because they had stepped back, or because they hadn't been there at all.

×

I waited for the bus to Mattie's, not caring that the rain was still drizzling down on me. I couldn't get any wetter than I already was. The warmth from within was keeping me from thinking about it too much. My thoughts switched from Cooper to Mom, seeing as it was getting so late, but decided not to bother texting her. Friday night was "date night." Landon and Mom would be out to dinner and a movie or play—Mom's new favorite pastime, now that she, or Landon really, could afford it. Henry would be with Landon's mom.

It may have still been September, but the late September rain often meant frozen fingers and blue lips. The warm feelings inside had thawed and the shiver set in by the time I reached Mattie's.

A different, cozy feeling met me at the door—his mom had the heat on. I sighed. But it wasn't just that. Mattie's was like a second home, and coming here always felt like a soft, welcome cuddle.

An hour later, at the kitchen table, I wiggled my toes on the chair across from mine. My homework was spread out in front of me, though I had only managed to disassemble and reassemble my pen fourteen times. I wrapped my hands around the mug of hot herbal tea Mattie's mom had set in front of me after I changed out of my uniform. But the tea had gone all tepid on me.

Mattie and Franklin were playing video games in the living room behind me. I turned around as it changed into a full contact event of headlocks and arm twisting. Their rumble spilled onto the floor in front of the couch. There was an explosion on the game screen and Franklin jumped to his feet with a victory howl. He flexed his muscles—impressive if it weren't for the freakish faces he was making. Mattie started beating him over the head with a couch pillow.

"I'm starving! Order me up a pizza, loser," Franklin barked to Mattie.

I turned to see Mattie getting his phone out. He texted us.

I expect cash money.

"I paid last time," I protested.

"Ha! Last year maybe," Franklin said. "Too bad we can't make Gav pay. Punishment for blowing us off all the time lately. He's getting as bad as Cass."

My head jerked up. "Where is Gav?"

"Don't know. Mattie thinks he's gone bi and got a secret crush at your school."

"What do you mean?" I asked, glancing at Mattie who was concentrating on our online order, or ignoring me, or both.

"Earlier in the week Mattie saw him with that brunette girlie again," Franklin said.

"Marilyn?" I tried not to sound too concerned.

He shrugged, like he was already over the topic. "How the hell do I know? Ask Mattie."

Mattie was still putzing. How much clicking does our usual two garbage pizzas take? I packed my books back into my bag. No way Gav was digging on Marilyn. I couldn't even see him being friends with her. Just ... why?

Something else popped into my head, which didn't help any.

"Have you noticed the new wheels on Gav's board?" I asked Franklin.

"Hell, yeah! They go with the new trucks he showed up with on his board this week."

Alarm bells were going off in my brain. Gav never got new anything. "Where'd he get them?"

"Stole them? I don't know. He won't tell. Wherever he got 'em, I'm gonna have him go get me some. They're sweet." He slapped his arms down to his sides. "You got that order in yet, fatty?"

Mattie did. Thirty minutes later we settled in with extra blankets and pillows—Mattie and I on the couch with heads on opposite ends, and Franklin stretched out on the carpet in front of us. Mattie turned on channel forty-four's *Zombie: Blood Lust* marathon, and we ate our pizza. The small black-haired zombie reminded me of Gav and the way he rolled up onto the balls of his feet when he walked. Like anything without wheels just felt all wrong to his legs.

I think I was the first to doze off, somewhere in the middle of part three. I was dreaming that zombie Gav chased me to my school, only to find that everyone there had already changed. I heard a buzz followed by two chirps. I opened one eye to see Mattie's phone sitting next to mine on the coffee table, both screens lit. Gav was batch texting us. Who else would it be?

I thought real hard about reaching for the phone. But Mattie's mom stepped on Franklin as she threw another blanket on top of me and Mattie. Then it was all over. Sleep was already pulling me back down. Whatever it was could wait.

I was wrong.

Chapter 9

Mattie's foot knocked into my ass from the other side of the couch. I yelled and gave him a kick, causing him to flip onto the floor. I looked over and realized he hadn't landed on Franklin. Franklin was gone. Mattie came up laughing with his cowlick sticking up like a sideways mohawk. I reached to tame it, but my phone was beeping on the table so I went for that instead.

I checked for new texts as Mattie headed for the kitchen. I found the one from two o'clock in the morning from Gav. It said:

I got trbl

I looked over to Mattie who had one hand in a

frosty flakes box and the other on his phone. Our eyes met. He shrugged.

I dialed Gav, but his phone went straight to voice mail. I texted Franklin asking him where he'd gotten to. He sent back that he was at Gav's.

Gav in trbl? I sent.

No answer.

Whatever it was, maybe it blew over.

I pit-stopped in the bathroom, doing my business and washing my face. I pulled open the medicine cabinet and found my toothbrush Mattie's mom got for me when I stayed over.

Back in the living room, Mattie handed me a toaster pastry and a Coke. I chewed as I threw all my stuff back into my bag. I looked over and saw that Mattie's mom had folded my uniform and hung it on the back of the dining room chair. One sniff told me everything. She had washed and dried it. My socks, too!

"Can your mom adopt me?" I said. "Seriously?"

Mattie smiled and hooked his arm around me, dropping a kiss on top of my head.

I'll adopt you.

"Sure, but do you do laundry?" I started to push him away but he held on. Being best friends with a boy, especially someone like Mattie, required certain rules, certain unspoken boundaries, a line I had to tiptoe. It wasn't something we discussed, but something

we both adhered to. The hug was only a couple seconds longer than what I'd usually allow, but enough
to make heat snake up my neck. When he did let go he
wouldn't look at me. I stood stock-still and waited. If
he wanted to talk about . . . anything . . . it was for him
to bring up. *Not now*, I thought. *Please not now.*

He tipped his head toward to door. *Let's go check
on Gav.*

×

The road was slick under the wheels of our boards, but
at least the rain had stopped as we headed down to Rice
Street. I leaned back on my board and swerved around a
puddle to avoid resoaking my still damp shoes.

Gav's half sister, Greta, let us in and greeted us
each with a hug, a practice I never got used to. All her
girly girl crap made me feel like looking for an exit.
I found Greta useless for mostly anything, always
smelling of weed and flirting with Franklin. Which
was just gross. I mean, Franklin is hot looking—he'd
be the first to tell you—he's great for a laugh, and
he's not a bad guy. But it's gross because he was way
younger than her, was her brother's friend, and he was
Franklin—someone who French-kissed the bottom of
an ash tray because some guy bet him twenty bucks.

Greta led us to her room, which was pink. A serious
pink with trinkets and dollies everywhere. This must be

what ad nauseam meant. Her thrift-pick furniture was pushed against all four walls, leaving the center open and covered with a braided rug of rainbow pastels and flat pastel throw pillows to sit on. I'd seen those pillows last year in a bin at the dollar store. This colorful sitting space had to be where she passed the bong with her friends. No one could stand this room sober.

The whole situation was weird. We never hung with Greta.

"He's in the bathroom," she said as I opened my mouth to ask about Gav. I still wasn't sure what exactly was up, but I decided to go with it.

After her insistent patting, I lowered myself next to Greta on the pastel green pillow. She took a long drag off her cigarette and smiled. I glanced back at Mattie who had given up on his pacing. He rejected the pillow invite and began fingering Greta's knickknack-lined shelves.

"Everything cool with Gav?" I said.

"Dunno. He didn't come home last night." She smiled and blew out three smoke rings and watched as they drifted away.

"I thought you said—"

"Franklin. Franklin's here." She smiled again, then snapped forward. "I know, right? Franklin isn't even supposed to be in my room—at least not when my dad's not home. Not after the last time—"

"Greta—"

"We had sex. A lot."

I heard a tinkle of glass breaking behind me and turned to see Mattie crouch down, scooping up what looked like two halves of a unicorn figurine. Greta's low chuckle brought me back around and I had to hold her wrist still to keep her from ashing on my pant leg.

Talking to Greta was like talking to my senile grandmother. On acid.

"That's . . . gross. What about Gav?" I said.

"Are you sleeping with Gav? What about Mattie?" said Greta, the queen of random.

There was another crash behind me and I didn't even turn. I pulled the cig from her fingers and dropped it into her pop can. I was two seconds from shaking her when Franklin burst into the room.

"Did you tell them?" he asked Greta.

"About us?" she asked.

I stood up and broke in before anyone could bring up sex again. "Somebody talk to me. Not Greta."

Franklin grabbed the remote from Greta's bed. He looked sidelong at her with annoyance. "Why'd you turn it off?"

When he pointed and clicked we all turned to see the TV mounted on the wall. It was shiny and flat-screeny and out of place in the room full of secondhand furniture, garage sale knickknacks, and childhood memorabilia. Mattie whistled his appreciation.

The Channel Nine reporter chick who Franklin referred to as "Titspatrick" was standing in a field with trees sectioned off by yellow DO NOT CROSS tape behind her. She pointed to a stone path lined with tooth-shaped rocks—

I knew that path. "Turn it up," I said.

". . . late last night. The body has been removed from St. Bernadette's in St. Paul, but crime scene investigators are still working the scene."

"A body?" I asked no one in particular as a chill tore through me.

Franklin answered. "Dead guy was found in the woods behind your school. His head all beaten to mush."

I whipped my head around. He went on. "Swear to God, not making it up. They showed the picture on the news, and it was one of the assholes from the other day. The blond one. Cooper something."

"Shut the fuck up," shot out of my mouth. It was all that came out. I couldn't think. My heart was beating so fast at this point it was painful. But no other part of me was moving. I couldn't remember how to breathe.

Mattie was tugging insistently at my elbow. *Cass, Cass, Cass.*

I shook him off. My ears were getting hot.

Franklin was talking to the room at large. "Not that I'd, you know, want anyone dead, but that guy was a total asshole. Am I right?"

I launched myself on him. He toppled over, bouncing off the bed and onto the floor with me on top of him. He blocked my swinging fists with his hands, but I wasn't through. I wrenched one of my wrists away from his grip and got a good hit at his face before he had a hold on me again. Mattie grabbed me around the waist and hauled me off. I kicked my feet out as he pulled me away, catching Franklin in the thigh.

"What the hell? Chain your bitch, Mattie!" Franklin rubbed his leg where the blow landed.

I tried to go for him again but Mattie's yank on me sent us both backward onto the braided rug. When my breath hitched in my throat I realized I was crying. I pawed at my eyes but found them leaking out faster than my fingers could chase. Mattie pushed out from under me and started pacing and pulling on fistfuls of hair.

"You're a fucking liar. You fucking lie, Franklin," I said. My whole body shook like a seizure. I pulled my knees up, let my head fall forward, and gave up resistance against the flood. Greta wrapped her arm around me as I rocked uncontrollably.

"It's not true. It's not," I said, more to myself than anyone.

"It's okay, Cass, we're all just post-traumatic stressing is all. It'll pass," Greta said.

I thought about punching her, too, since she and Franklin were barely stressing, let alone feeling post-traumatic anything. But I couldn't find the energy, so I didn't fight her off when her other arm did its snaky wrap thing and hugged me.

I lifted my forehead from her shoulder when Mattie threw open the window by the bed. I was thankful for it, as the oxygen content had shrunk in the room. Franklin was busy not moving. He had that quiet stillness boys get whenever a girl cries. I knew they both must be freaking because I'm never that girl. This wasn't me, but so much of the last weeks weren't me.

I focused on my breathing. I needed to get a hold.

Titspatrick was back on TV. I was so busy looking at the picture of Cooper in the corner of the screen that I missed the first part of her report.

". . . do not think robbery was a motive. A 'person of interest' was taken in late last night in the regards to the death of Cooper McCay, the eighteen-year-old senior here at St. Bernadette's, whose death is being called 'suspicious.'"

I felt like my whole body was turning to stone. It was true. Cooper was—

"Suspicious? That's an understatement. What, he bashed his own brains in?" Franklin said.

I shot him a warning look as Greta *shhh*ed him.

Titspatrick continued. "Police are not calling him a suspect at this point, but we can tell you this 'person of interest' is also eighteen, so we can reveal his identity to be that of local Gavriil Ivanov, who attends—"

The room erupted in swears and groans. Greta was on her feet. "Fuck. Fuck. Fuck."

I glanced over to Mattie, still leaning on the window sill, looking stock-still at the TV.

His eyes locked with mine.

TRBL was right.

Chapter 10

I stepped onto Landon's Welcome mat. When I'd left, Greta was trying to figure out how to get a hold of Gav's dad. Flaky as he was, there wasn't much choice with their mom, Who-Knows-Where.

I stood there looking at Landon, Mom, and Henry. No one looked at me.

Mom had QVC shopping network on. Her feet were up on the ottoman with cotton plumped between each toe. The room reeked of nail polish. Landon sat next to her with a baby name book, and Henry was on the carpet with his cars.

He made sound effects of brakes screeching and crashed the cars into a terrible wreck. "And then you die," Henry said.

"Shut it, Henry!" I said. It came out in an angry whisper, my throat aching from holding back the sudden threat of tears.

"What's wrong with the name 'Molly'?" Landon asked Mom, oblivious to Henry and me as usual.

Henry, as his usual, was oblivious to the break in my voice that would indicate I was upset to anyone who was listening.

"Then they go to heaven," Henry said, without looking up.

"Not Molly," Mom said to Landon. "Where've you been?" Mom asked, and I realized she was talking to me. Her tone was merely conversation-like, not like she was actually concerned about me being unaccounted for. I broke my gaze from Henry and his cars. Her eyes were already back on the TV as she rubbed her tummy bump. She had a faraway smile that had nothing to do with me.

"Mattie's," I choked out.

"Girls sleepover?" Landon asked, cracking himself up. Mom swatted at his arm but was still smiling. I dropped my bag and hung up my coat. They both had settled on the assumption last year that Mattie was gay. Which was twisted since they had no clue about Gav. I guessed it was how they justified my and Mattie's sexless relationship, since I'm sure neither one could fathom being friends with someone of the opposite gender without boinking them.

How little they knew about my life. I didn't have to lie because they couldn't be bothered to ask. Even as

I stood there on the worst morning of my entire life, tears filling my eyes again, I couldn't earn a glance.

Look at me.

"The heat's on," Landon said to Mom.

"Close the door, Cass," she said to me.

"How about Peyton?" Landon asked Mom.

I slammed the door.

"Did you slam the door?" Henry said.

"Yes, I slammed the door." I tried to keep my voice steady.

My feet felt like fifty pounds as I heaved them upstairs. My mom's voice froze them in place. "Some kid at your school died. Cooper McCarr or something? You didn't know him, did you?"

My arm started to shake where it death-gripped the banister. "I don't have any friends at that school."

When Landon spoke, his voice was low like the conversation was directed just at Mom. "Sounds like some kind of fight gone bad."

"Like there were fights that went good?" I mumbled.

"Shocking at St. B's, though," he said, but not to me.

Whatever. At least they didn't seem to know about Gav. They must have clicked off before that.

"It's sad," Mom said to Landon. But she didn't sound sad, just distracted as she rubbed that beach ball–shaped lump under her shirt again.

A low "hmmm" from Landon in response, and that was it.

I wanted her to ask. Ask me if I was okay. Ask me if I wanted to talk. I wanted a mom who gave a shit when I didn't come home all night. But that wasn't going to happen.

I hated her with every step I took up those stairs.

At the threshold of my room, my arms drooped uselessly at my sides. My eyes scanned the room. I felt Cooper all around me and it was making it hard to exhale.

I could see him there. The careless slack of his uniform pants. The clean lines of his undershirt beneath his uniform shirt. Not a wifebeater, but a proper white tee. He rolled up his sleeves, transforming from buttoned-up school boy to casual hanging mode. The muscles in his forearms were tanned and unexpectedly sexy.

I sat down on my bed as I did the day he was here and "watched" as he stood there, at my dresser, picking things up and putting them back down. He chatted on about each item, turning to comment about one of the bands I found worthy enough to have a poster of tacked on my wall. He saw them in concert, would you believe, with his older sister. He took in each pinup above my desk, ripped from my skater mags, and asked questions about the trick being performed. What it was called, and if I could do the trick myself.

He smiled at me. And when he moved toward me on the bed, every touch was deliberate and slow in case I wanted to stop him. But I didn't. We weren't there too long, jumping apart when my mom called, letting me know when she'd be home. We moved down to the floor and pulled out our books to study, though it's impossible to concentrate on American history after having someone's tongue in your mouth. That's when we'd had the talk about his mom having cancer. And how people . . . leave.

The memory dissolved and tears rolled down my face. I opened my jewelry box—a present from my grandma Rossi—which didn't hold any jewelry but instead personal treasures. As soon as I flipped the carved wooden cover I could see the picture of my dad. He looked intense. Young and styling. On the prowl for a good time, that was my dad. But in that picture there was something more, something behind his eyes. Like sadness. Like an apology. At least that's what I chose to believe. I loved him in that picture and hated him in real life. I flipped Dad's picture over and behind it sat the instant pic of Cooper. I thought again about the day in his room. After taking my picture Cooper insisted I take his. He looked at the camera like he looked at me. Like he was looking deep in me and trying to sort out the puzzle that was deep inside.

I couldn't take him looking at me like that. I slipped the picture into my pocket. With me, but away. I flopped onto my bed, mashing my face into my pillow. I could still smell him on it. Feeling a need to be away from all of the memories, I stood and picked up my iPod from my bedside table. I pulled up a hardcore playlist, one that wouldn't give me a chance to think about him.

I pulled off the blankets from my bed. I stared at the pillow and considered leaving it, but the pull was too strong. I tucked it under my arm and went straight for the only place in the room that didn't hold memories of Cooper: my closet.

I turned the music up as I made a nest against the pile of dirty clothes. My phone buzzed against me and I pulled it from my pocket. Mattie. I ignored him. He was a basketcase when it came to emotions—even other people's. His sensitivity was one of the reasons others like my stepfather questioned his sexuality.

I was the broken one. Always the one stuffing emotions away, with Mattie right next to me sweating emotion through his pores. He's always been like that. The only funeral I've seen him at was my uncle's, who Mattie had met once. Yet he was so overcome he ran out and vomited in the bushes, the retching continuing for ten minutes straight. It was everyone else, he said. He soaked up their emotions like a sponge.

I put my phone back in my pocket, but then pulled it out, turned it off, and slid it across the floor.

I gave it a last look, sitting half under my bed, before pulling the door closed.

And the day was gone.

×

It was late—dark, anyway—by the time Mom thought to check on me. It wasn't out of concern; the boys were beating down the front door for me. She looked at me in my nest with a furrowed brow.

"Something wrong with your bed?" she said.

"No," I answered. Ask me. Ask me what's wrong.

But she didn't. She rolled her eyes at my apparent teen ridiculousness. "Well, don't be loud. Henry's already in bed and Landon is reading."

I'd been in a closet the entire day, but she was more worried about my potential loudness.

"Right-o. We'll keep our drama down to a kitten's whisper."

She shot me a look, but still didn't have anything to say.

"Well? Send them up," I said, climbing to my feet.

I edged around her and ducked out to the bathroom to take a pee. Splashing water on my face, I caught sight of my reflection. My eyes were bright red with dark shadows below. My tone, pale even on a good day, was ghostly. I gulped down water out of the cold tap. My stomach rumbled, reminding me that the sugary breakfast was long gone. But I was about fifty-fifty on whatever I ate would actually stay down. I pressed my face into a bath towel and rubbed the fabric into my cheeks to bring back some life to my face.

When I got back, Franklin and Mattie were standing around waiting. I was so very pleased Greta wasn't with them, though not pleased they were looking all shifty with their back-and-forth glances. I shut the door.

Mattie tossed me a fast-food bag. I swear he was just as thoughtful as his mom.

Without pretense, Franklin jumped in as I unwrapped the burger. "Hey. Was that guy . . . were you guys, like . . . ?" Franklin said with an awkward flapping hand gesture.

I took my time chewing my first bite. This would be the time. But the lie came easier than the painful truth. I swallowed.

"Don't be stupid. It's not like that. He's dead, Franklin. You just can't joke about some things."

Franklin slung an arm around my neck and gave me a wiggly headlock that passed for a hug in our world. "Sorry," he said. "But I am so happy you weren't fucking him. I really hate those guys."

Mattie sat down on my bed and didn't say anything. He leaned over and picked up my phone off the floor and handed it to me.

Franklin released my head. "We got a prob. Before we could send out a search party to all the bars and strip clubs, Gav's dad called Greta back. Cops told him Gav was picked up by your school right after the body was found."

"Cooper," I snapped. "Can we just—? The guy's name is Cooper. Was . . . I mean was."

Franklin bit off part of his thumbnail and spit it onto my floor. "Right. Whatevs. They found Gav a block off Snelling. As soon as he saw the cops, he started beating cheeks."

"He ran? Idiot! What the hell was he even doing by my school?" I asked.

"No clue. They caught him, obviously, and they saw the blood on his board."

I felt a stab of fear. "From the fight?" I instantly hated that it came out as a question.

Mattie nodded and made an action with his hand exploding from his nose.

Blood everywhere.

He kept his eyes on me too long, gauging me. I took another bite of my burger, even though my stomach was clamping down around it.

"Right," Franklin said again, bringing my attention back to him. "Gav's dad said they can hold him for three days—not including the weekend—until they have to book him or release him."

"If they think he did it, why don't they book him now?" I said. "Frogtown kid in Highland Park after dark? Isn't that a crime?"

"They're building a case. Trying to figure out the whys and whens and hows and all that shit."

"Is he . . . in jail?" The thought made me panic.

"He's fine, he's not in Stillwater. They're just holding

him in St. Paul. They're not going to plop him into a cell with murderers."

"They think *he's* a murderer!"

He rolled his eyes. "When the pieces don't fit, they'll have to let him go. When Gav's mom shows back up, she'll—hey! Wasn't your mom dating a lawyer?"

"That was like, two years ago for about five minutes, and all he handled was living wills and tax forms and crap," I said.

"Well, whatever. Three days, not including the weekend, so they have until Wednesday before they have to release him. It'll be fine. They got nothing."

"Nothing? Franklin, he was arrested within a block of the crime scene with Cooper's blood on his skateboard after threatening to brain him two days before."

He shrugged. "Motive is weak. Everybody hated that guy."

"Nobody at my school hated Cooper."

"How about the killer?" he said with a smirk that I wanted to knock off his face.

But his statement shut me up. I'd been so busy concentrating how they'll find out Gav wasn't the killer that I hadn't given much thought to who it could be. "It could've been anyone, right? Could have been a random . . . homeless junkie?"

Franklin made a buzzer sound. "Wrong. News said he still had his wallet on him. This was personal." He moved to the door. "I'm outie. Gonna meet up with Greta so I can do some consoling. You coming or what?" he asked Mattie.

Mattie shook his head.

Franklin stood halfway in and halfway out of my room playing with the doorknob. "Cass?"

"Yeah?" I said through my last bite of burger, hoping it wouldn't be making a return appearance.

"Another good thing about not messing around with that guy . . . ?"

Cooper, I wanted to say again. "What?"

"Cops are always looking for the love triangle motive with teen murders. It's always jealousy." He thought for a second. "Or drugs."

"According to what?" I asked.

"TV."

I rolled my eyes, but had to think about the drugs. I hated that I had to even consider Cooper was maybe right about Gav dealing drugs. Drug dealing and a rap sheet. Here we go. Way not to be a stereotype, Gav.

The door clicked behind Franklin.

After tossing the grease-soaked bag in my trash, I went back over to my closet to grab my pillow. I clicked the remote and the nineteen-inch TV on my dresser came on. It used to sit in our living room where my dad and I would watch the Twins in the summer—back when he was still around. It was nothing like Greta's flat screen. Maybe she'd had a birthday? Their family had nothing.

Nobody in their neighborhood could afford that. Well, not legally. Her new TV was weird, and it bugged me. Dealing drugs? The pieces would fit, but I didn't want them to.

I bumped the volume low. My head was swimming as I crawled over Mattie, who was already settled against the other pillow. Fucking Gav. The weight of the thoughts caused my eyelids to become unstoppably heavy before I could even set down my head. I rolled with my back to Mattie.

I handed back the remote. "Don't leave me, okay?"

I felt the mattress shift. The only contact he made was his fist tapping my shoulder once.

Never.

×

In my dream I was in the woods behind school. The changed leaves had yet to fall, but they lit the trees on fire with their reds and oranges and yellows, even in the dark. There was a snapping of branches and I whipped around, stepping down in something wet. I looked down and saw two things: I had forgotten my shoes, and I had stepped in blood. The blood led off in a neat trail through the dirt, deep into the trees. I didn't want to follow the trail because I knew where it would lead.

I took a step back when I heard it. The voice was all around me. "Help," he said. Cooper's voice cracked as he said it, like it hurt him to speak. "Help me, Cass." My name was drawn out into a hiss. I circled, but there was no right or left. Every view was the same. His voice kept saying my name until there was only the hiss all around me.

I opened my eyes and realized that Mattie was shaking me. His face was two inches from mine. He tapped at my face with his fingers.

Wake up. Wake up. Wake up.

I was trembling so bad that I decided it was better not to talk. I nodded to let him know I was awake and that I'd heard him. He rested his head back on his pillow sliding his forehead against mine. I closed my eyes. My breath hitched as his hand rested on the side of my neck, his fingertips just under my hairline under my ear, causing goose bumps to erupt over my thighs. I held my breath for a second, wondering if he was making some kind of move on me.

I opened my eyes to peek at his face. He'd dozed right back into his soft snores.

I wasn't so lucky. Sleep was not my friend.

Chapter 11

I woke early. Even without rolling over to look at my clock I could tell that it was early. The house was quiet, and the sunlight through the window was soft. The biggest clue was no morning cartoons blaring from downstairs yet. I lay there and stared at the wall. I could hear Mattie's soft snores behind me. I could feel his foot against my ankle.

My thoughts drifted to Cooper. I thought about the look on his face Friday—I couldn't believe that it was only two days ago—when I told him we were through. I'd gone back and forth so much in the last couple weeks it was like relationship whiplash. I was glad I'd made up with him again, but it was maddening we never got the chance to give it a go. It wasn't fair.

I burrowed my face in my pillow. I didn't want to move. It wasn't even today that I was dreading so much, because maybe there were a million things I could do to block it out. Tomorrow morning would be a thousand times worse. I'd have to face St. Bernadette's knowing that Cooper wouldn't be there. He was the one bright spot in the darkness. Every single fucking thing would be a reminder, another slash in my skin, a painful reminder of what I had.

I slept as long as I could. When I finally did get up, it was because my bladder was demanding it. Mattie was gone and I felt a little betrayed, until I found him in Henry's room, with Henry, playing *Lego Batman* on the Wii. I plopped down next to Mattie, close enough to feel his muscles flex in his arm as he played.

They finished out their level and Mattie handed over the controller and pulled me up by my hand. Henry didn't say anything as he switched it over to one-player mode.

Mattie and I grabbed our boards and left through the front. Landon was in the garage. I swear his head came up over one of those paper masts as we passed, but as I lifted my hand to wave, he turned away. We stopped at the bakery across Snelling Ave. for deli sandwiches. Instead of heading south on Snelling past my school to the skate park, which would be our usual on a sunny day like today, I led Mattie north on Snelling, then east up University past every block in the old neighborhood. I kept on until my thighs burned and breath came out hard from hitting every green light. When I looked up we were at the Capitol building, with its golden horses on the roof. I veered off to the grassy area behind the Capitol where all the suits had their lunch during the week. Today there were families flying kites and some kind of picketed protest that only had about ten people.

We ate our sandwiches in silence under a shady tree. As I finished the last two gulps of my Coke, Mattie was lying back, his arms butterflied under his head, the breeze ruffling his hair. His eyes searched mine and I knew he had questions about me and Cooper. But I wasn't ready for his questions. So I just laid my head on his arm and closed my eyes.

Tomorrow would be the day for questions. Today was the day for quiet.

×

Monday morning, I kept my music on during breakfast. Through the bass beat I heard Landon's cereal bowl clatter down onto the counter. He pointed repeatedly at the TV next to the toaster. Gav's face was posted behind the anchorwoman, his eyes looked hollow. Mug shots always had a way of making someone look like, a criminal. The picture then changed to Cooper. He was smiling in last year's yearbook shot—same as the framed one in his upstairs hallway—that had him looking more alive than Gav. I swallowed hard on the tasteless bran lump my cereal had become.

Landon had stopped his frantic pointing and stood there looking at me. I took my bowl over to the sink and turned on the tap, hoping the next story would be grand enough to steal his attention away. As soon as I had the water filling my bowl, Landon had a grip on my arm. He yanked my earbud out.

He pointed at the TV again before finding his voice. "That was the twitchy Russian kid you hang out with."

My eyes veered to the window. I wished I could get by with a shrug.

"On the news," he prompted.

I nodded and pulled my arm away.

He leaned in. "They said murder," he said in a low voice, as if "they" could hear us in the kitchen.

"He didn't do it," I said.

He stepped back and rubbed his palms over his face before finally calming down enough to talk to me. "What's going on? Do we need a lawyer?"

"I don't know anything more than you, except I know Gav. He's a shit magnet. I'm positive it was a 'wrong place, wrong time' kind of deal," I said.

He looked me over. "But you didn't know him? Cooper McCay? That's Thomas McCay's son." He said that like it was supposed to mean something.

I shook my head.

He blew out a breath. "This is why I transferred you."

"Why? Because you knew Gav would one day be wrongfully accused of murder?"

"No, because you need to find friends impervious to shit."

Problem was, seeing as Gav was innocent, there was a definite possibility that I was going to school with a murderer. At St. B's. But I knew this train of thought was beyond my stepfather, who was incapable of believing anything bad of his alma mater. I nodded and kept my mouth shut.

×

School was a joke. A sad and twisted joke that made me want to beeline for the toilets to empty the bran mush from my stomach. People had actually made banners and armbands in a macabre attempt to socially display their grief that seemed more like a competition than a genuine expression.

The banners were up on either side of the doors.

STUDENT COUNCIL WILL MISS COOPER one banner said.

RIP FELLOW PEER COUNSELOR COOPER MCCAY another declared.

Cheerleaders were sobbing loudly on the front steps of the school in front of the press. I mean bawling. Mascara running. It was an embarrassing mess.

Two girls who looked like freshmen were giving an interview to Channel Nine News about what a "nice guy he seemed like."

I turned away from the spectacle and my eyes went to the grass that leads to the side of the building, and all the way to the woods. I felt drawn to the place that was ours, even with Cooper gone. Or maybe especially with Cooper gone. I felt drawn to the one place that could make it real. I needed to look. I needed to see.

I checked around to make sure no one was noticing me, but as usual I was invisible. My heart was beating so hard in my chest I was afraid others might be able to hear it. At the corner of the building, I could see across the field. There was police tape stretched all along the woods on either side of the paved path. Just like I'd seen on the news. The path itself had two wooden barriers set up and cops standing guard. A couple more were squatted down, one of them pointing to something on the path.

It happened there. Somewhere behind that tape they found Cooper. Dead.

My helpful imagination conjured up an image of what Cooper would look like dead. Pale and still and bloody. With the side of his head . . .

The bran mush was coming up. I made it behind the bushes next to the wall . . . but then the urge subsided. My eyes rimmed with tears. I felt the sweat break across my hairline and dabbed it with my sleeve as I turned and started to find someone standing there. It was Black Glasses, from the locker across from mine. But his glasses were in his right hand, his left wiping furiously at the tears that fell freely. He doubled his efforts with both hands when he saw me looking at him.

I wiped my sleeve across the sweat and tears on my face and swallowed. "Are you okay?" I asked, forgetting my own sadness in the face of his. Crying always makes someone look younger, and he looked like a kid. A six-foot-tall kid.

"Yeah," he said. He sniffed loudly, shoving his glasses back on his face. Both lenses were smudged from his hands and tears. "How embarrassing," he mumbled.

I felt a pang of pity at this genuine emotion. I suppressed the urge to clean his glasses and help put him back together. But that wasn't my job. "You don't have to be embarrassed because you're sad. It's like, human."

"I just don't want people to think I'm like one of those cheerleaders on the front steps," he said.

"You don't wear enough eye makeup for that."

"Well, luckily not today." He sniffed. "You don't have a . . . what's a manly version of a tissue?"

"Sorry. I'm not girly enough to need them."

"Except today."

I dabbed at the corner of my eyes again with my fingertips. "Yeah. Except today."

"Me too." He sniffed again and I turned away as he used the back of his hand to dab his drippy nose.

"It's shocking," he said.

"What?"

"It's a shock. The police. The tape." He indicated with a tip of his chin. "Makes it real."

Not wanting to get into the realness or anything else with him, I mumbled a quick, "better go," and walked around the front and into the school.

Inside near the office, I noticed that the poster touting next Friday night's bonfire and pep rally for Homecoming now had an added blurb about how the function was dedicated to Cooper. I stuffed a piece of gum into my dry mouth.

A crowd had gathered around Devon. People were patting him on the back as they passed. He nodded and gave out solemn fist bumps. I didn't see Eli.

The teachers seemed to be stumped about how to handle a school in mourning. After the announcement in homeroom, and the offering that extra peer counselors, the district's psychologist, and social workers would be available for anyone who needed them, we went on to our classes as normal, though it was obviously anything but. Some teachers did their best to carry on, but even Sister Rita gave up pretense and declared free study time after the chicks in the back row burst into tears after the bell.

Free study basically meant hushed conversations about Cooper and speculations about what he was doing in the woods.

Good question. I selfishly hoped he wasn't meeting up with Marilyn. Not that it mattered in the long run.

About halfway into the period, still lost in my thoughts about Cooper, I realized Sister Rita was staring at me. I tried to shake it off and pull out my textbook, but I couldn't even pretend to read.

When the bell rang I packed my bag as fast as humanly possible and pushed through the crowd. As I reached the threshold of safety in the hall, Sister's voice rang like a bell behind me. "Cassandra. A word, if you please."

I stepped back so that everyone else could pass. It was only when I was two feet away from where she sat at her desk that I could look at her. She wore a dark green sweater, and her hand was already resting on her chest over the top of her dangling crucifix. She removed her half-moon glasses and I was startled by the sadness there. She licked her lips.

"I've known the McCay family for a long time," she said.

I nodded, not sure what else to say.

"It is very hard to understand when God takes a child from this earth, his family, and . . . loved ones, especially in such a violent way. I keep praying for understanding and for strength and for healing. I will pray the same for you."

Her hand moved from her cross and I was sure for a moment she was going to reach out to me. Instead, her hands clasped together on her desk. "You may go, Cassandra."

I nodded again. She never before seemed so sisterly. And so human.

For French, we had time in the library for our study project. I was supposed to be looking for something on Joan of Arc and how she rocked all kinds of battles, but I was mostly just zoning out until I spotted Marilyn in the World War II section. Two other girls were with her. One was hugging her, the other patting her shoulder.

"I'm like, so sorry, Lyn," one said, flipping her braids over her shoulders with a twist of her head.

"He was sooo cute. It's tragic," the other joined in, releasing her from the hug.

The way they were treating her like the grieving widow was like adding salt in the wound. It twisted the knife. As the girls finished their good-byes and slipped away, I sidled up. I didn't have a plan, but I had a burning need to put her in her place. Marilyn was reaching for a book on the top shelf.

"Marilyn?" I said.

"Aaah!" she gasped dramatically, clutching her chest. The book crashed onto the floor. "You scared me."

Drama queen. I reached down, picked up the book, and handed it over. "Sorry. I'm Cass. I was . . . a locker neighbor of Cooper's."

She looked me over and then flipped her mane of hair over her shoulder. "He never mentioned you."

I bit my lip. "No? Well, I just wanted to tell you how sorry I was to hear about Cooper. You guys seemed close."

"Yes. Very," she said, without a blink or a stutter.

"You were . . . very close?"

"Yeah, we had a thing. It was no secret," she said with a shrug.

I had been expecting an allusion, a hint, not a *boom!* full-out admission that blew a fresh grenade of pain in my chest. She looked at me while I regrouped. "So, you knew Gav, too, right? That kid they say killed him?"

"I didn't know him. Why would you say that?" She looked me straight in the face, unwavering. If I didn't actually know she was lying, I wouldn't know she was lying.

I stepped closer. I lowered my voice like we were sharing a secret. "I saw you with him. Gav. And that whole thing last week with the drugs? I heard Cooper telling Eli. That must be awkward?"

"Stay away from me. It's not—I don't—that's really rude." She banged past me, dropping the book on a table on her way to the stairs.

Only two things were clear: one, I really did not like her. And two, I honestly couldn't tell if she was lying about her and Cooper.

I thought about her admission. *We had a thing.* Suddenly it seemed imperative that I knew. That if Cooper was real with me.

I climbed the steps the way she'd gone, through the belly of the library to the upper level. There was a stream of people cutting both ways through the upper level. Taking a chance, I went right since Freshies and sophomores were located on that side of the school.

I pushed my way through the door to the hall and spotted Marilyn halfway down talking to a guy with a shaved head. He looked about the same build as the guy Gav had been talking to that day after school, but it was hard to tell without seeing his face.

"Hey!" I called. "Excuse me. Dude?"

Marilyn's eyes flashed over his shoulder and she said something out of the side of her mouth that looked like *GO.* She peeled away and entered a classroom on the left side of the hallway, but I wasn't interested in any more of her lies. The guy took off straight ahead, and with his long-legged advantage, he doubled his lead on me.

"Hey!" I called out to him again. "I need to talk to you!"

At the far end of the hall there was another staircase, which he took down. I followed him as fast as my legs would carry me. When I reached the second-floor landing I looked up and down the hall. Back at the stairs I leaned over the bannister to see if I could get a glimpse of him below.

Gone.

×

At the end of the day, I joined the crowd exiting through the front door. I'd told Mattie I'd meet him at Kellogg. Depending on what Eli and Devon were telling everyone about Gav, it would not be cool for any skaters to show up at school. At the bottom of the steps the crowd wasn't splitting up as it normally would. Instead, nearly every-one was moving right, toward the field.

Devon was at the front giving some kind of speech with his back to the police tape. He held up a white wooden cross, where a school tie was fixed around the neck. "This is for you, Coop," someone said next to Devon. I lifted up on my toes to see it was Eli. And then Devon bent down and disappeared.

I assumed he must have driven the thing into the ground because the crowd broke into applause, and two drama queens next to me began to wail in each other's arms. I slipped around the side of the crowd and inched my way forward to get a better a look at the taped-off section of the path as it disappeared into the trees.

I thought about Cooper deep in the woods under a tree. All alone on the damp, cold ground. Bleeding. Did he die right away? Or was he bleeding and disoriented in the woods trying to crawl his way out to get help. Did he have his phone? Did he try to call? I swallowed.

"Weird, huh?" a voice said to my right.

I snapped my neck. Black Glasses. What the hell was his name? Brandon? He was leaning toward me.

I rubbed the side of my neck as he continued. "I just can't get over it. Like he's here one day, and the next . . ."

I nodded. There was no way I was finishing that sentence for him.

A sound like a jackhammer caught my attention. There

was a group of guys working along the path behind the tape.

"What are they doing?" I asked.

"Maybe getting samples of the concrete? I imagine they're going to be working until they have every sample of blood, hair, whatever."

Why were they working over there? Wasn't the body "pulled from the woods?" I was sure that was what we'd heard on the news.

"Did you hear about the memorial party?" Black Glasses caught my attention again. "It's Friday night at Kella Lambert's digs. You know Kella, right?"

"Uh, sure." No idea.

He smiled. "You'd probably know her if you saw her. Maybe?"

I shrugged. "I guess I'm not very social."

"I've noticed. Life's too short, though." He pulled out a flyer from his bag and handed it to me.

Across the top it said something about "Drowning your sorrows." And then a map that had a house circled just off Grand Ave., not far from Cooper's house.

"Thanks," I said.

He smiled. He had great teeth. Straight, but with a tiny space between the top two.

I smiled back. There was no way I was going.

The crowd was breaking up, moving in groups back toward the front of the school. I drifted along with them. Outside the front door, at the top of the steps, a cop in a suit was talking to Headmaster Spanders. The cop's tie was covered in limes—the fruit.

I hung back pretending to fight with the clasp on my bag. Especially with Sister Rita and her staring, I wondered if I was going to be on a list of people to talk to. I don't really like to talk to cops about anything if I can help it, and I sure as hell didn't want to be talking about me and Cooper. Not today. Not ever.

Spanders's mustache twitched as he pointed. I turned my head to see Devon and Eli coming around the corner of the school. Spanders called out to them. I turned my back to Eli and Devon as they passed. I had to hear what they were going to say. Were they going to tell the cops about the fight with Gav? About the drugs? As they mounted the steps to meet Spanders and Limey, the cop, I scooted forward and dropped down along the stone wall that lined the steps.

Above, Limey accepted introductions and apologized for their loss. Then things got interesting.

"I heard that Cooper and you boys got into it with some skater kids at Luther Park last week. Could you tell me about that?" Limey asked.

"Skater freaks. The Indian guy, the little black-haired guy, and the blonde girl . . . they don't like us, we don't like them," Devon said.

"So you know them?"

"No. They don't go here."

"So what happened?"

"It was just a thing. But it ended with that black-haired guy—the one that killed Coop?—threatening to smash his head in with his skateboard."

"How did it start?" Limey asked.

"I think one of them threw the first punch. The Indian one I think. But I can't be sure, it all happened fast," Eli said.

"Why were you fighting?" Limey said.

There was a pause where I can imagine them exchanging glances, then Devon is talking again. "You guys already know all this, don't you? And you got *the guy*. So what's with all the questions?"

"It's an investigation." Limey left it at that, and when the silence stretched out long enough, Devon continued.

"It just happened. Name calling, then pushing. And then it was on."

"Who's the girl? The blonde?"

There was a pause. I held my breath until I heard his answer. It was me he was talking about. "No. I'm not sure who she is. I think they all must go to Kellogg," Eli said.

"Any idea what Cooper was doing here at school the night he was killed?" Limey asked.

"No idea. We were at the Flame. Everyone was there like usual. Cooper got a text. Then he was out," Devon said.

"He didn't say who he was going to see?" Limey asked.

"I don't know, man. I was kind of distracted. My girl and I were fighting," Devon said.

"What were you fighting about?"

"That part of the investigation?" Devon said with a slight snip.

"Just trying to get the details of how the night went down for Cooper."

"It didn't have anything to do with Cooper. It wasn't even a fight. Hailey was in a rotten mood, PMSing I guess, and it got me in a rotten mood, you know?" Devon said.

Whether Limey did or did not know wasn't clear. "What about you? Catch what the text was about or who it was from?"

There was another pause. "I assumed . . . it was a girl? But he didn't say," Eli said.

The pauses seemed weird, like Eli was thinking too long about something. I was so preoccupied with thinking about his pauses that I missed the next exchange about Cooper leaving.

"What time did you three leave the Flame?" Limey asked.

"Pretty much right after Coop," Devon said.

"In the same car or . . . ?"

Now they were all quiet, as I assumed the guys realized their alibis were being checked.

"No. Eli had his Rover. I dropped off Hailey and drove home," Devon said.

There was a silence, then Eli jumped in. "Drove out right after Dev. Went home. Parents were asleep."

"All righty. Thanks guys. If you think of anything else,

here's my card," Limey said. "Might need to do some follow up."

×

When I arrived at my old school Mattie rolled my board toward me and I stopped it with my foot. I reached up to tighten my hair band. Mattie grabbed my wrist and brought it down in front of my face.

Where's your bracelet?

Where? Good question. The last time I'd seen it, it was heading into Cooper's pocket. But if he had it on him when he died, that certainly would have warranted some checking out. With my initials c.z. engraved on the charm, it wouldn't have taken much detective work to track me down at St. Bernadette's.

Mattie shook my arm to get back my attention.

"I don't know," I said. The lie came fast. It wasn't as if I wasn't already sure that Mattie knew about me and Cooper. He knew enough. But general knowing wasn't the same as saying something out loud.

Mattie watched my face, then started to shake his head.

You know.

I opened my mouth to let a little truth out, and shut it again when I saw Mattie press his lips together. His eyes were over my shoulder. Limey came up and flashed us a badge. "Hello, skater kids. Would you happen to be friends of Gavriil Ivanov?"

Chapter 12

Limey was fast. Finished with Devon and Eli, he was then on to tracking down skaters from Gav's school. He seemed pleased with himself. He took down our names and asked for Franklin's name by description and I gave it. He took me aside after learning about Mattie. Didn't want to take the time with a mute. Not many did. My plan on the fly was to be honest, but not get Gav into any more trouble than he was already in. Because lying to save a friend is totally different than lying for personal reasons.

"You go to this school?" Limey asked.

A checkable fact. "No. I go to St. Bernadette's."

He raised an eyebrow. "You knew Cooper McCay?"

"Yeah. Everyone knows him. Knew. Knew him," I said.

"Were you two—?"

"His locker was right by mine," I said, figuring it was better to volunteer something safe.

"Were you friends?" he asked.

"No. People like him are not friends with people like us."

"But at private school you're all the same, aren't you?"

I hesitated. Was he having me on or was he an idiot? Uniforms didn't wash away social inadequacies and differences. He was smirking. I didn't laugh.

"No, we all just look the same," I said. "Like cops."

His smile dropped and we moved onto the run-through of the fight. I told him I didn't know why they jumped Gav. Not sure at that point what advantage it was to give him over as a possible drug dealer, even if it did open up other suspects. I wasn't even sure what was up with all that yet. It wasn't the time to volunteer something that would just make it worse for Gav.

"So it was just random violence? Come on. Did Gav hit on Cooper's sister? Spit on his hundred-dollar shoes . . . ?"

I shrugged again. "Why don't you ask his friends? They jumped us."

"I did." He looked back down to his notebook. "Did Gav threaten Cooper?"

I wanted to lie. I would've lied if I thought I could get away with it. But he had it from Eli and Devon already. Better to downplay. "Yeah, but it wasn't serious. We were just dumbing around. It's not like it's a gang thing, we're just from different sets. Preps and skaters, jocks and T-birds, greasers and socs."

"Right. That's why I'm trying to figure out if it was your Johnny that killed the soc."

Crapsticks. "Forget *The Outsiders*, what I'm saying is this wasn't a bloodthirsty situation. We all had a laugh with Gav about it after. No biggie."

"Gav wasn't holding on to any feelings of a missed opportunity?"

Nice one. I held his gaze. "Why would he? We won the fight. Cooper was the one who left bleeding. All over, in fact. Gav had it on his jacket, his pants, his skateboard. . . ."

The cop narrowed his eyes. Too quick? "Your friend Gav was caught on a bloody skateboard, fleeing the scene of a murder. The victim being the same kid ol' Gav had threatened two days before. I just need to fill in some blanks, and your buddy can start working on his defense."

Shit. I'd pissed him off. "He didn't do it."

"How do you know?"

"There's no reason. They didn't even know each other," I said.

"No? Well, they both knew you, right?"

I held his stare again.

"Locker neighbors?" He said, stepping in on me. I held my ground.

Mattie's board slapped down on the concrete behind me.

The cop sighed. "Pipe down, Harpo," he said to Mattie.

Limey snapped his notebook shut and straightened his tie. "That's all I need. If you think of anything else . . ." He handed me his card. "Give one to Silent Bob, too. He can . . . text me."

Chapter 13

Okay, so I'd lied to the cop, at least by omission, about me and Cooper. But it wasn't any of his business and had nothing to do with Gav. The guy obviously wasn't even looking for other suspects. He was just looking to connect the dots. I sure as hell wasn't going to help him do that.

I ran my finger over the official-looking seal on the card. I thought about tossing it, but slipped it into my wallet instead.

Mattie glanced at his watch and shrugged.

What's next?

"Cooper's house," I said.

He blinked at me, not following along.

I kept on before he could protest. "Cooper had my bracelet. Plus, there must be something. Some clue as to who he was meeting or what he was into."

He kept on with his staring. I stood perfectly still and let him stare. Sometimes I could totally understand why Henry felt more comfortable without eye contact. Cooper having my bracelet admitted something. It raised a lot of questions about how and why, which could only lead to more questions—none of which I wanted to answer right now.

Finally, Mattie dropped his gaze and waved a hand in the direction Limey had gone.

But the cops—

"They probably gave it a once-over, but you heard Limey. They're only interested in things that will help them sew up Gav," I said. "They weren't looking for my bracelet, and if they had it, they would have matched it to me. And . . . I want it back."

×

We approached Cooper's house from the alley. I motioned to Mattie and we stashed our boards in the bushes next to the garage. Behind the garage, an oak's branches twisted up to the back of the house. I glanced around, but remembered Cooper mentioning that most of his neighbors were DINKs—double income no kids—and not rich enough to have maids or anything.

I glanced into the garage through the side window and saw that it was empty. While I thought it was too soon for his parents to be back at work, I hoped it meant that they were gone. I headed toward the back door with my head down, but kept my stride strong like I belonged. No creeping around, or we'd just look . . . creepy.

When I reached up and got the key from the ledge above the door, Mattie gave me a funny look, like how'd I know? I just shrugged and ignored the burn on my cheeks. I leaned my head close to the glass and listened. Nothing. No voices, footsteps, TV, nothing. I slid the key into its slot. Mattie reached out and placed his hand over mine on the key.

"For Gav," I said, and took a moment to convince myself that it was true. That it wasn't more about my need to find my bracelet. Before I could back out, I turned the key.

The door blessed us with the absence of a squeak. I listened again as I counted to four before stepping inside. I pulled the key out and knocked into Mattie as I leaned back to replace it above the doorframe. He gave me a gentle shove into the house.

I glanced around the kitchen and headed up the stairs. My feet hesitated on the way down the hall. Mattie moved ahead of me; he didn't have to ask. The car posters and general lack of order we could see through the open doorway gave away the teenage boy's room. He pulled drawers, shifted socks, lifted shirts.

I kept my teeth clenched as I peered in and instantly felt Cooper all around me. The smell on my pillow was a drop compared to the tidal wave that overwhelmed me. It was like five Coopers from my memory inhabited the room. In the game chair, stretched out on the carpet, sweeping a hand during the grand tour . . .

My teeth began to chatter and a wave of anger made me clamp down my jaw. Had Marilyn been in here with him?

It took me a minute to collect myself behind Mattie's back.

Cooper's desk had been cleared off of all the junk. In the junk's place was a manila envelope with a pile of things underneath. I pinched the corner of the envelope and lifted it off. A wallet, four pennies, a ring of three keys, smoothed-out receipts from the Flame, and Gas-N-Go. The wallet was unfolded and I could see the tops of Cooper's DL, student ID, and a credit card. I could also see the tops of some cash peeking out the very top. I'm sure the cops had emptied it all out, so I wondered if Cooper's mom or dad had taken the time to file it all back in. I flipped over the manila envelope and there was an itemized list of what had been inside—what had been on Cooper the day he died.

So no robbery, and definitely no bracelet.

I set the envelope back on top of the pile and thought of my own hiding spots. I moved back over to Cooper's bed and checked under his pillow, holding my breath to avoid the smell as I ran a hand underneath, then inside the pillowcase. I turned to see Mattie open the other door: the closet. I pulled back the curtain to check on the sill when I heard it. A door slamming below us.

I spun around, but even as I went to grab Mattie there were footsteps coming up the steps. I stood still and told myself there would be no reason they would need to come in here. No possible—

Mattie yanked me inside the closet. Once I caught my balance, I turned to see Mattie ease the closet door closed behind us, leaving just an inch open, not risking the click.

The bedroom door creaked open. I crouched next to Mattie to peek out, our combined breathing sounding like a wind tunnel.

I could see a woman through the crack, and I assumed by how old she looked that she must be Cooper's mother. Her hair was blonde like his, with the same mouth and nose, but different eyes. She was scanning the room slowly, but she didn't have the crinkled look of suspicion. Only the blank slate of mourning.

I watched as she looked around his room at all of his things. Cataloging. Probably noticing details for the first time. Taking an interest in parts of him she'd never found interesting before. She reached over to his desk and picked up his Minnesota Twins cap. As she turned it in her hands, I could see the inside liner was frayed and stained from his sweat. This set her off. She clutched it to her chest and her face crumpled until the tears leaked out.

Mattie shifted a couple of times next to me. I sunk onto my knees and rested my head against the doorjamb. It felt like a movie, watching her there on the bed. She was so consumed by her grief, I thought we could have walked right out of the room without her noticing.

I don't know how long we were like that. Her rocking with his hat, and me watching. But when Cooper's mom's sobs quieted and she pulled his bedspread over her shoulder, my own face was wet. I turned and Mattie was gone. I even looked up to the ceiling for answers before my eyes adjusted to see there was another door on the far side of the closet.

I peeked out one more time into the bedroom and saw that her breathing had slowed. I turned the knob completely and eased the door shut without a sound. The closet was pitch black as I walked through, counting three, four, five steps before my outstretched hand reached the other door.

I turned the knob quietly and pushed. Inside was Cooper's bathroom—and Mattie making good use of his time. Enough daylight was coming through the blinds to allow his search. Currently he was digging through the medicine cabinet. He pulled out Tylenol, contact solution, razors, shaving cream, and bandages.

I started to put the items back. But as my hand reached for the bandages, Mattie snatched them away. I rolled my eyes at his digging around until he pulled

out a picture. I made a grab for it, but he held it out
of my reach and got his eyeful before handing it over.

It was the instant pic Cooper had taken of me in
his room.

"Thanks," I whispered, without looking at Mattie. For
some reason I felt like the picture couldn't have revealed
more if we'd been naked. His eyes stayed on my face
trying to find all the answers there, but I wasn't going
to give him anything else. I wasn't ready. I squirmed
under his look, sliding the photograph away into my
pocket with the one of Cooper.

We finished our search, and when I was halfway
through the closet, I heard rustling back in Cooper's
bedroom. I wasn't sure if she was cleaning, trashing, or
looking through the room. But I was sure that Cooper's
mom was no longer sleeping.

Chapter 14

I motioned for Mattie to go back into the bathroom. With the door shut behind us I was looking at the ceiling again for an escape hatch, but all I saw was a fan the size of a cheeseburger.

I peeked behind the blinds, which only reminded me that we were still on the second floor. I'm not real good with distances, but I knew it was high enough up that we'd break our legs jumping.

I brushed past Mattie and back to the closet door and pressed my ear against it. She was still going at it. Cleaning, I guessed, as it sounded like books and things being dropped into boxes. We had to hurry or the closet would be next. I went back into the bathroom where Mattie . . .

wasn't. How could he possibly keep disappearing on me in such a small space?

I brushed the blinds aside and got a face full of fresh air, followed by a size-ten shoe. I looked down to see that there was a decent-size ledge, then looked up to see that the roof must have been fairly flat, because Mattie was now sitting on it with his arms stretched toward me. He clapped his hands.

Let's go.

"You can't be serious," I said through my teeth.

He smiled, but there was something nasty in that smile. He was challenging me.

I wiped away at beads of sweat forming on my forehead. I knew I was going to do it. Cooper's mom couldn't have been scarier to me than if the room had been full of pacing tigers.

I stepped up onto the sill. The window frame was nearly tall enough so I could stand up straight within it.

Mattie pointed to the gutter fastener next to his right foot, then two bricks on his left that stuck out more than the rest. Balance was not a problem. And strength? Better than average, I'd say. But the distance between me and the ground, and the added pressure of being caught by Cooper's mom and the police made my knees wobbly.

I grabbed on to the gutter as I shifted my feet around. I was about to lift my foot to the brick when I thought about leaving the place as I'd found it. So I edged back and used my foot to ease the window closed. I glanced up at Mattie who was watching, but no longer smiling. He reached forward to get ready to assist, though it wasn't at all clear how he was planning to do that.

I swung my leg up to plant my foot on the brick when I was reminded how much shorter my legs were than Mattie's. My foot biffed and caught nothing but air. The momentum left me swinging for a second before my feet found their way back to the ledge, which was a lot thinner now that the window was shut.

Mattie had his hands around my wrists, but I shook my head. I had to be able to switch my grip or grab for him when I needed to. I rubbed my face against the shoulder of my sweatshirt where the sweat was moving down my cheek.

This was it. I'd have to do it in one go. I glanced up to see if Mattie was ready. He nodded. I swung my left leg hard and used my stomach muscles to propel me. As soon as my foot hit the brick, I kicked off of it, using my arm muscles to guide me up. I wouldn't have quite made it on my own, the angle was all wrong, but as soon as he could reach me, Mattie had me by the front of my sweatshirt and hauled me the rest of the way, my knees scraping along the gutter. We lay there for a minute, me half on top of him, remembering how to breathe.

We both knew where we were going—the oak by the garage. We set off single file along the dip where the two peaks met. I must have been crawling too slowly for Mattie, because he kept ramming his shoulder into my butt. We reached the peak and I invited him to go first. The crazy oak was nice enough to have grown right next to the house, and even despite trimming, there was a sturdy enough branch to step onto, with several more to take us down without any more impromptu gymnastics.

It was almost dark when we collected our bags and boards from the bushes. I was thankful for my picture, though still wondered about the bracelet. But what swam in my head was the image of Cooper's mom crying. I knew this wasn't just about Gav. This was about Cooper. No matter what went on between us—fake or real. No matter what kind of guy he really was—asshole or saint—or if I should hate him, or if I could have fallen for him . . . this was about Cooper.

Chapter 15

We limped our way back to Gav's. Well, I limped, Mattie walked. I felt the blood from my scraped knees dribble down my legs into my socks as I went.

Back at Gav's, I sat on the pastel green pillow and scowled at no one in particular. I was annoyed we found ourselves in Greta's room again. But seeing as she was here, and Gav . . . wasn't. So be it. But damn if her cigarettes weren't keeping me on the edge of crazy. She was cleaning up the cuts on my knees and applying the biggest Band-Aids ever, taking her time blowing smoke rings in between. I kept prodding her on her visit to see Gav, since right now only family was allowed in. But she seemed intent on telling us everything useless about the downtown station where they were holding Gav.

"It wasn't, like, dingy, but the walls were gray. Gray is the saddest of all of the colors."

"Greta—"

"Oh! And before we could go in they patted us down and took my purse and shook it out. I'm talking ciggies and tampons everywhere." She peeled off the backing and stretched the Band-Aid over the cut on my left knee.

I pulled the second one from her hand. "Did you talk to Gav?"

"Talk? Well, kind of. Mom was blubbering, his dad was yelling. It was a scene. The usual," she said.

I slapped the Band-Aid down on my right knee hard enough to make myself cringe. I spoke slowly. "What . . . did Gav . . . say?"

"Oh, you know. He's innocent. Blah, blah."

I was going to have to punch her. I looked wide-eyed to the boys for help. Franklin jumped up from the pink pillow. "I think maybe you were right, Cass, especially after what you said about those assholes pinning the fight on us and making Gav look like a loose cannon? I think they're going to charge Gav," he said.

I had given them a quick rundown of both the conversations—the one I'd overheard with Devon and Eli, and the one Mattie and I—well, the one *I* had with the cop. "Thank you, Mr. McObvious."

"I think we need to do something. We need to find out who did it. No way we can rely on the cops to do it if they think it's Gav."

I looked around and saw Mattie nodding and even Greta seemed like she was following.

"Any ideas?" Franklin asked.

I smoothed the Band-Aid on my knee, figuring that was as good of an opening as I was going to get. "This is dumb, but I overheard that Devon and Eli"—I really needed to stop lying—"and Cooper jumped Gav because they said he was dealing weed at St. B's. I know, it's crazy stupid"—I said before they could interrupt with protest—"but Gav was spending a lot of time at St. B's and meeting up with people?"

"Damn! That's where he got those new trucks for his board," Franklin said.

"Wait. For real? You just believe it?" I said.

Greta let out a huff. "That shit. I knew my stash was dwindling! I thought maybe the kids were getting wise at Midway Elementary."

"You stash your dope at the elementary school?" I asked.

"No, it grows there. Under the trees by the back fence. Gav was with me one time when I got some."

"Bet that's where he got the money for your TV," Franklin said with a smile.

Greta shook her head. "Shit-bot. That was for personal consumption only."

I sat back. "He didn't need that stuff."

"Easy for you to say, living the good life with Step-daddy Warbucks," Franklin said.

"It's Landon's money, not mine."

"Whatever. Maybe for once Gav wanted something nice for him and Greta."

"But dealing drugs? Didn't we always say we didn't want to be the neighborhood stereotype? No gangs, no drugs, no baby momma drama?"

Franklin shrugged. "It was just weed, Cass. Another year or two it will probably be legal. He was just cashing in."

All I could do was shake my head. Gav never would have done that before. But now I wasn't so sure. Gav had never felt the need to impress anyone with fancy things, if that was even what he was doing.

"Did you know?" Franklin asked Mattie.

I was about to interrupt again because, of course, Mattie didn't know—when Mattie nodded. "What?" I said. "Seriously?"

Mattie nodded again without looking at me.

"He told you?" I asked him.

Mattie shrugged then mimed zipping his lips.

Franklin nodded. "Yeah, you can keep a secret. Fuck. It's like we're all living a bunch of lies." Franklin's eyes were on me. "So is that what the assholes were telling the cop?"

"Um—No. I just heard it. People talking about Cooper and defending someone from Gav the 'dealer.' A Freshie."

"Who?"

"Her name is Marilyn. That brown-haired girl we saw Gav with outside school. She sort of, maybe had a thing with Cooper."

"If we are going to do this? If we are going to find out who killed that guy? No more fucking lies. We have to be in this together," Franklin said.

My throat tightened, but I swallowed past it. There was no reason they had to know.

I caught Mattie looking at me. I looked away.

"Where do we even start?" Greta said.

Franklin groaned and fell back on the bed. "There could be a million reasons why people hated him like we do," he said. "Too bad you're not fake friends with any of them; it would be nice to get the down low on their social deals."

I felt into my sweatshirt pocket and pulled out the flyer for the memorial party on Friday night and opened it up for them to see. I cleared my throat. "Would this help?"

Chapter 16

When I got to Mattie's on Friday, Greta was already there, which made me feel funny. But even more ha-ha funny was the look of fear Mattie had as I came through the door. He pulled me by my sleeve and rolled his eyes toward Greta, who was freestyle rapping to herself in the kitchen.

Help.

I could only help by absorbing some of her conversation after she broke off her song. We headed upstairs to raid Mattie's brother's and sister's closets—his brother already moved out and lived in Minneapolis, and his sister was away at college on a full-ride scholarship. Mattie's sister was three years older, his brother four years older, and both had wardrobes that were American

Eagle throwing up on Abercrombie & Fitch. Mattie was the rebel baby of the family. It annoyed me, too, because I could see Mattie's mom having to pull extra shifts at the hospital to pay for this brand-name crap. Mattie was all thrift. But I guess they were used to their fancy things. Money wasn't such an issue when they were young. They did all right with his mom's income until Mattie had his bout of cancer. They had medical insurance, most nurses did, but long hospital stays and radiation appointments made it hard for Mattie's mom to work much at all.

Now that Mattie was better it seemed like she was constantly working doubles and overnights and whatever she could to keep up on the bills. I've never heard her complain about it. Opposite really. It's like since Mattie was sick, she just wants to do whatever she can for them. But I think what Mattie really wants is for her to be home more. He doesn't say so, of course, but I can tell.

I pulled on an outfit of what I thought was "passable preppie" and went to sit in the bathroom as Greta applied makeup on me. I didn't even punch her when she curled some of my hair. I avoided the mirror on my way out and waited downstairs for Franklin who was going to pick us up in the "getaway car"—whatever that meant.

I was pretty sure that because Devon and Eli hadn't ratted me out to Limey or the school as the skater chick from the fight, they hadn't made the connection yet. I was banking on not running into them tonight at all if I could help it. Even if they did see me, they'd be more likely to recognize me as the girl who had a locker next to Cooper than anything else. Maybe.

Greta and Mattie had insisted on going. I didn't like it. Greta was fine, nobody knew her. But if Mattie was recognized, it'd be like having the murderer in the eyes of Cooper's friends. He shrugged me off. He'd do what he did best: be invisible.

I got up from the couch when I heard Mattie thumping down the stairs.

Greta looked back and forth between Mattie and me. "All righty then, Mr. and Mrs. Tan Slacks," she said.

I glanced down to see that Mattie and I were both wearing khaki pants. "I'm changing," I said, but before I could make a break for the stairs, a horn honked outside. Greta opened the front door and there was Franklin, his arms wide, swinging around to proudly show off his . . . mother's red minivan?

"Are you cracked? The minivan?" I said. "That's the 'getaway car'? That thing predates boy bands."

"Hardly. Besides, it's more about suburban camo than speed. Minivans are everywhere," he said, looking kind of hurt.

"Not piece-of-shit minivans," I said.

Franklin ignored me. "Everyone got their phone?"

Franklin didn't accept our nods and wouldn't move on until we all showed them.

"Good. The code word is 'redrover,'" Franklin said.

"That's two words. Red. Rover," I said.

Franklin glared at me and Mattie's shoulders started to bob.

"Whatever," he said. "You get the group text for *Red Rover*, it means Asshole One and/or Asshole Two are spotted, there's trouble, or I have to make a sandwich run."

"Why do we care if the assholes are there?" Greta asked.

"Because they might recognize Cass and Mattie from the fight and not take it too kindly that Gav's friends are slumming at their memorial."

It was true, but I was banking on us blending in. They hadn't taken any notice of me so far at school because it was easier to dodge them there. We couldn't risk one of them putting two and two together.

"We all good?" Franklin said. "Wonderful. So we keep our ears open and work on the list."

I pulled out the list we'd compiled of our "Persons of Interest." I was pleased it was short and not some massive organization involving half the school.

1. Marilyn.

Of course Marilyn. She knew Gav. She was *whatever* with Cooper.

2. Tall guy. Head shaved with the funny teeth. With Gav at St B's. Possible buyer?

Number two was vague for the others, since I was the only one who'd seen him, so I'd have to make him my goal.

Franklin reached around me with a pen and added:

3. Asshole One

4. Asshole Two.

Then wrote because he's a douche next to each.

"Devon and Eli? Because you think they know something or you think they might have . . ."

He merely shrugged, like that would explain it all.

He didn't need to like them. I didn't like them, but his flippant attitude at the news of Cooper's murder wasn't forgotten. "I know I said they didn't have alibis, but that doesn't mean—to be fair, why would they kill their best friend?" I said.

He shrugged again. I restrained from grabbing those damn shoulders.

"I'm just saying, keep your ears open for any beef between them and Cooper. You never know what assholes are going to do."

"Like kill their best friend? This is real in your mind? Or are you just being a dick?"

He looked at me like I was small and silly. "Let's just keep an open mind."

Franklin was an idiot. This was the exact moment, just as my blood pressure was rising and my fists clenching, that Gav would usually jump in. Mediate. Crack a joke.

Do something stupid to distract us. But Gav wasn't. And this was infinitely worse than any other time.

"*And*," Franklin was going on, "Greta can chat people up looking for random angles and motives, because Greta does random better than anyone," Franklin said.

Greta smiled like it was some sort of compliment, though maybe from Franklin it was.

×

Franklin drove in an uncharacteristic silence. He let us out a block away and we hoofed it from there. The party looked like it did involve half the school. Maybe more. We separated at the curb, Mattie disappearing in a casual stroll around the back of the house where I could hear the party had spilled out into the backyard. I grabbed Greta's elbow.

"Just tell people you're Emma's cousin," I said.

"Emma who?"

"Just say 'Emma.' Or 'the blonde Emma.' They're like a dime a dozen around here."

She nodded and lit up a cigarette. A smile creased her lips as she inhaled. "Kind of exciting, right? Partying with a killer? I loves me some danger." She peeled away up the path and through the front door.

The air felt heavy. I didn't want to be there.

I reminded myself of my role. We were locker neighbors. I had a casual interest, at best. Better yet, I'd just ask about drugs. Smooth. My feet started moving and pushed through the door. That blonde from my home-room—I think her name actually was Emma—was making out on the front room couch with a tuba-player guy. I've seen him lugging that thing around school. Scattered around the room were groups of kids talking, like it didn't bother them that Tuba was about to get to second base right in front of them. A couple of them glanced over at me and gave me the once-over. Nobody smiled, nobody waved. Not that I was surprised, but this was going to be harder than I thought.

"Hi, you," someone said, and I felt a hand on my arm.

Shit. I turned. A girl with massive braces was smiling at me. I knew her. Kind of. Gym? French? She yelled over the music. "I know!" she said before I could come up with anything to say. "We look so different in real clothes. I love your top!"

A piece of spittle collected on her lip from getting all those words across all that metal. I glanced away from the spittle, trying to think of something to say. Above Tuba and Emma was a peek-through wall and through it I could see the kitchen.

"Yours, too," I said, but she was already turning back to hug a lanky girl on the fringe of a pack of crying girls. It took me five minutes to wade through them toward the kitchen. When I found my way out, I was faced with a smiling Cooper. Bile reached my mouth before I could swallow it back down. There was a poster, on a stand, full of photos of Cooper. Probably fifty of them, all centered around the most amazing life-size headshot.

I knew that smile. I recognized that twinkle. I forgot to breathe.

"Hey, girl." Some short and stocky type was beside me with his sweaty hand on my arm, hot beer breath in my face. "It's gonna be okay. Need someone to talk to? Shoulder to lay your head on?"

I brushed his ham fist off me. "You're using his death as a line?" He opened his mouth to protest. "Don't. Just . . . don't," I said. I couldn't keep the shake out of my voice. His smile dropped and he turned, disappearing into the crowd, but it was with a shrug. Like it was me who had the problem. Tears sprung to my eyes.

I tipped my chin down and tried to get a grip. I had to. As far as tonight was concerned I was just a locker neighbor, I told myself. But my mind wouldn't listen. All I could think of was the intense way Cooper's eyes would lock on me and the way he made me feel. Squash it. I had to squash all that shit or I was seriously going to lose it.

On the floor next to the poster was a giant bucket filled with ice and bottled beer. I grabbed one out by the neck, pushed back through the flock of girls, and turned down the hall. Through the second door I spotted a bathroom and I went in, slamming the door behind me. I twisted off the beer cap and chugged as fast as I could.

I pulled back to take a breath and let out a burp. My hand was shaking as I pulled out the instant pic of Cooper from my pocket. After a glimpse I shoved it back and had to jam my thumb and pointer finger into my eyes in an attempt to plug the tears. But with my eyes closed I could feel his hands on my back, his lips on my neck. I sunk down onto the toilet seat. Then the track changed, like on a CD, and he was gone. He was really gone. I opened my eyes, loathing the pastels and seashell-shaped soap. Fuck these people. Fuck these clothes and these preppy curls in my hair.

Then I was on my feet and my fist was smashing into the tiled wall. A soft knock at the door made me jump. "Hello?" some girl called. I ignored it.

I examined the blood dotting along my knuckles. The sting was enough to chase thoughts of Cooper away for a while. And that felt good. I even thought about repeating it, but I wasn't drunk enough for that.

A bang came from the other side of the door. "Come on! No making out in the bathroom. I gotta pee."

Making out? I wish. I wasn't much of a drinker, but getting shit-faced and hooking up was sure sounding good. My brain even dared to flash on Mattie and a heat rose in my chest.

What was I thinking, coming here to find a killer? If I stayed at the party sober, eventually breathing would take too much effort.

I drank the rest of the beer down in another three gulps and tossed the empty bottle into the dainty pink trash bin next to the sink. I ripped off a few squares of toilet paper and blotted it against my knuckles before tossing the wad down on top of the bottle.

I swung open the door. Two girls were standing so close I could smell their makeup.

"Sorry," I said as they stepped back. "Contacts." I pointed at my eyes—which were no doubt red and puffy.

I made my way back to the kitchen. There was a tall guy facing the window above the kitchen sink. On the counter I spotted a cup full of something dark and wet. My mouth was dry and bitter, so I grabbed the tumbler and began to chug. It was sickly sweet and tasted like flat root beer. I was fully aware this could possibly be laced with battery acid, but I didn't care. I swallowed it until it was gone.

The tall guy turned around. Black Glasses. Behind the glasses his brow was pinched. "That was Ziggy's root beer," he said.

I held a hand to my forehead and tried to figure out if the nausea was receding, then I lifted my chin to look at him. "Sorry. I'll get him another one."

Greta's familiar laugh bubbled over next to me, but I kept my eyes pinned to B.G.

He smiled. "No, it's just—it's fine, Cassie."

Instant guilt. I hated when people knew my name and

I didn't know theirs. "Okay," I said, but it came out like a question.

Greta laughed again. I shot her a glare.

His voice brought me back. "You look great out of your uniform." His smile dropped. "Not that I—or that you're—I don't know. I mean . . . you probably do but—"

I let him stammer and tried to think of his name. A name. I'm sure I knew it. Byron? Bryan? Braaaaa—

He was shaking my arm. "You okay? You know that was mostly schnapps, right?"

"Schnapps. Right." So that's what was boiling in my stomach.

"Try this instead." He handed me another bottle of beer and I started drinking it right off.

Through the window I could see the fire burning in the fire pit in the center of the yard. I scanned and didn't see Eli or Devon. Marilyn? It was hard to tell. Place was full of brunettes. I recognized Mattie even from behind. He was sharing a deck swing with a girl. A brunette.

Greta nudged me; I'd forgotten she was still there. "Righty. Well, off to stake out the potty." She smiled at B.G. "Perfect spot to catch guys with their fly down."

I turned once more to the backyard to check on Mattie, still sitting next to the chick. I whipped off a text: **Who dat?**

He glanced at his phone and put it next to him without answering. Then, as smooth and natural as I'd ever seen him, I saw him slip his arm around the girl.

The girl said something and he pointed to his neck. "Cancer." I mouthed along with him and watched as she reached out to touch the scar across his throat. I had the urge to bat her hand away. Here he was getting in his first moments with this girl, and I realized I'd never had that particular moment with Cooper. Never a sitting-on-a-porch-swing-with-your-arm-around-me moment. And we never would.

I jumped when a hand went on my shoulder.

Black Glasses was still there.

"What?" I said sharply.

"Sorry," he said, pulling his hand back with a jerk. "I was concerned. You seemed lost for a sec."

I shook my head. "Fine. Just thinking about Cooper." I flinched. I hadn't meant to say that. But it was normal, right? Even if we were just locker neighbors? There was an ache in my throat. I closed my eyes and felt a tear slip down my cheek without warning.

His hands felt warm on my shoulders. When his forehead brushed along the side of mine on the way to a hug, I cut off the movement or any pending words of sympathy by pressing my lips against his. He froze for one very scary second, and then his mouth started to move against mine.

I was aware of every voice and movement around us. My head spun, but I was sure it had nothing to do with the kiss, because my body was numb. I tilted my head back, breaking the kiss.

"Thanks," I said. My cheeks flamed with heat. I mentally smacked myself. What kind of idiot thanks someone for a kiss?

B.G. blew out a breath and bobbed his head in a nod as I wiped any remaining wetness from my face. Depending on my own emotional stability was becoming a crapshoot.

I scanned the room instead of working for awkward conversation. I spotted him. Shaved head, funny teeth: The dude I'd seen with Gav. He was standing by two other guys, both in football jerseys.

I leaned in to B.G. "What's that guy's name? With the shaved head? I forget."

B.G. turned his head. "Jesse? Jesse Gobston. The third."

"Gobston?"

"Yeah, yeah. Everyone calls him Gobbers. We're like, best buds," he said.

"Why?" I asked.

He paused, looking confused.

"I mean why do you call him that?"

"I don't know. We just always have."

"Is he . . . does he . . ." I tried to think of a way to ask if Gobbers was into drugs. B.G. was watching me. Waiting.

I heard the front door open and a lot of cheerful greetings. I turned and could see Eli and Devon had just entered. I jerked my head back around. B.G. was still staring at me, one of his eyebrows raised in question. I pulled my phone out of my pocket. I had to warn Mattie about Eli and Devon being here. In my haste, my fingers felt like sausages. My phone flipped out of my hands and skidded across the kitchen floor.

I bent down on all fours and followed it, weaving in and out of legs as I went. I spotted my phone lying on the ripple between the linoleum of the kitchen and the wood of the hall. I reached out my fingers just as someone in jeans stooped and picked up my phone.

Eli, still crouched, looked up from my phone to me and smiled. "Looking for this?"

I reached, and just as my fingers closed around it, his smile drooped. His grip didn't loosen. I pulled and his fingers fell away, but he continued to stare. My phone vibrated. I looked down to see that Franklin was texting **Red Rvr**. No duh. I rose to my feet using the wall for balance. I turned away from Eli. I smiled broadly at B.G., who had followed my crawl. I grabbed his arm with both hands.

"Brian, I have to go," I said.

"It's Brady," he said.

Fuck. But he was smiling. "Can you walk me out?" I said. I glanced around and saw the patio door. I tipped my head. His smile grew and I hoped this wasn't party slang for making out in the bushes.

Chapter 17

Brady held an arm out to steady me as I made my way down the back steps and stumbled.

"All right?" he asked, setting his hands on my hips when we reached a plateau of flat concrete. To my right, a blotchy-faced brunette was calling out her number and Mattie was dialing.

I squinted. Holy crapness. It was Marilyn.

Her phone chirped until she turned it off. They shared a quick little smile that had my jaw clicking. Then I remembered Brady, who was watching me again.

"Brady?" I said.

"Yeah?"

The question about Marilyn, if there was one, dried up

in my throat as I realized how close he was with his hands still on my hips. It was too much, and all wrong. "I need to go. I don't think I should've come," I said. I took a step back, but he took it with me like some kind of drunken waltz.

"Why? We're not all bad, you know."

My jaw clenched. "What about Gobbers? He a good one?"

"Yeah, he's great." His smile dropped, and so did his hands. "You're not into him are you?"

The ringing giggle caused my head to turn back to Mattie and the brunette. "I hate her," I said, not really meaning to say it out loud.

Brady turned to look. "What's going on?"

I checked back over my shoulder to make sure Devon or Eli wasn't coming outside. I studied Brady's face. I wondered whether I should trust the instinct to let my tongue wag, or go home and sleep it off. I hadn't scored a single lead, Mattie had only scored a date with Marilyn, and Greta . . . well, I couldn't hold my breath on that one.

"I've been doing some thinking about Cooper." My voice was so low, it barely came out. "What if . . . what if it wasn't that skater kid who did it? What if it was one of Cooper's friends?"

Oops. Maybe that wasn't very subtle.

Brady seemed to think the same thing, because he did a quick look-around as he led me away from anyone else. After another look-around he leaned in. "Cassie, you and alcohol don't work well together."

I laughed. Too hard. My stomach ached.

"You can't just show up at the guy's memorial kegger and start asking weird questions saying crap like that. If anyone heard you—"

"Gav didn't do it." Shit. I shouldn't have said that.

"Is that the skater?"

I nodded. I didn't even care.

"Then who did?" he asked gently, like a parent entertaining the wild stories of a four-year-old.

Tears were lining my eyes and I felt like I was four years old. "I don't know. It's not like I can talk to anyone here and figure it out."

When he didn't answer right away, I got distracted when I saw Mattie behind him. Greta flew through the screen door and jerked her head toward the side of the house.

Mattie came around to Brady's side and held out a hand to me. I ignored it.

I looked at Brady. "I have to go. Our ride's here." I indicated Mattie and Greta, who was either anxious or doing the pee-pee dance.

Mattie reached in and grabbed my wrist. I had to stuff the urge to snap at him. I was letting him haul me away, when Brady grabbed the sleeve of my other arm. I was caught in an awkward frozen tug-of-war between them.

"Can we talk later?" Brady said. He held out his phone to me with his free hand. I dug my phone out of my pocket and let him punch in his contact info, and I did the same with his.

"Let's gooooo," Greta said.

I patted Brady's arm. "Thanks," I managed to say. I pulled my hand back. Mattie didn't wait a beat before hauling off and half dragging me through the long grass at the side of the house. I glanced over my shoulder at Brady, and when I turned back I found myself pulled through a stubby bush between the house and the neighbor's wood fence. I managed to get a hand up to block the worst of it from shredding my face. My head was fuzzy as we came around the front corner of the house. I was two steps from the driveway when I heard a shrieky cry over by the front door. I stutter-stepped and my foot found a gopher hole.

My hand came loose from Mattie's grip as I was thrown forward and dove onto the gravel-covered driveway, my palms taking the brunt of the road rash.

Mattie stooped over me. He pulled back my hands to check the damage.

I turned my head toward the crying. There in the front yard was Devon, with his back to me. In his arms was a blonde, who I could only assume was his girlfriend, Hailey, with her face in his shirt and her arms clamped around his head doing her mewing and carrying on.

Greta was in my ear. "Are you okay? Are you okay? Are you okay?"

I pulled my wrists away from Mattie. The front door opened and Eli poked his head out, looking first at Devon and his girl, then over to us.

I planted my feet as Greta and Mattie each grabbed one of my arms and muscled me to a standing position. I watched as Eli's brow went from furrowed, then north into his hair as he took in our group. At the end of the drive, the red minivan screeched to a halt and the auto door eased open to swallow us up.

"Who was that?" I heard Devon ask behind us, his girl's crying calmed into sniffles.

I stepped up behind Mattie into the van and swivel-turned, leaning against the front seat for balance.

Eli was fixing me with a glare. He knew. He had to know who I was. Who Mattie was, too. But as the van door whirred to a close, I'm sure I heard his response and it made absolutely no sense.

"Them?" I heard Eli say. "No one."

Chapter 18

In the van, Mattie wasn't speaking to me. I may have made a crack about him scoring more numbers than leads, but it was a joke. Kind of. Greta broke the silence by telling the others about my encounter with Ziggy's root beer. Apparently it was the name of a cocktail, not the guy whose drink it was. They all thought this was hilarious.

"I'll pour him another one." Franklin repeated my line in a squeaky voice for the hundredth time.

When their laughter died down, Greta asked, "New hipster boyfriend, Cass?"

Crap. I was hoping no one saw the kiss.

"Hello? He's my in. The dude knows everyone. Including Gobbers—the shaved-head dude." I waved the list in her direction and noticed Franklin glance into the rear-view mirror at me. "I'll get Brady to help me, and then we'll run down the list. Simple," I said.

"That's what Mattie was doing," Greta said. "Dangerous Mattie, always one step ahead."

Mattie kept looking out the window.

"Maybe. I think he was just hitting on her because she's a vulnerable mourner," I said.

At least that's what I thought I said, but apparently it came out as "moaner" and it set them all off again into their fits. Except Mattie.

"Not sure if it's anything, but overheard some chicka-dees saying how fab it was that Cooper and Devon could 'make things cool again before Cooper died,'" Greta said.

I tried to blink away the fuzziness in my brain and focus. "When were Cooper and Devon not cool with each other?" I said.

"Dunno. I was all 'OMG, when were they fighting?' but they just looked at me like I was an alien," Greta said.

"You are an alien," I said, a laugh bubbling out.

"See, you never know what those assholes are up to," Franklin said as he pulled up in front of my house. He pushed the button on the ceiling and the auto door crept open after a few tries.

Franklin and Greta started laughing again about "moaning suspects" as I crawled out of the van.

Mattie still looked mad, but I poured on the puppy-dog

pout. I didn't want to be fighting with him and I didn't want to be alone. He rolled his eyes and lumbered his way out of the van to follow me. Franklin chirped the van's tires and was off.

Mattie wasn't looking at me. "Why were you macking on Marilyn? She's on the list. And don't give me some crap about getting info, I saw you with your arm around her and stuff." I felt like crying again. I wasn't sure why. "You could be putting yourself in with a murderer—a murderess," I said, pointing in his face.

Murderess? Really?

"Oh, make fun of me. Whatever." I started to walk away. He grabbed my arm.

You don't get to do that. You don't get to be upset with me.

I shook his hand from my arm and tried to school my emotions. "Fine. What do you . . . think?"

He pointed to his chest above his heart and winced. *Pain. She has a lot of pain.*

"From Cooper," I said, with a tone I couldn't help.

He nodded but indicated with his hand. *More.*

"More than just Cooper?" I shrugged. "Whatever. She's just high drama."

Mattie nodded vaguely but looked like he was still mulling it over.

"She lied to me about knowing Gav," I said.

He rolled his eyes. *Of course she did. Anyone would.*

Which, I guess was a good point. I didn't expect

her to pour her heart out to me. I probably would have lied, too. "Did she happen to mention an alibi while you were canoodling?"

He nodded. He used his fingers to mime hair coming down about three inches below each ear—like long pigtails or braids. I thought about the friends I'd seen Marilyn with on Monday. One of them did have braids. I nodded. But I wasn't letting go of my hate for her. Or my suspicion.

"Just be careful, okay? I don't trust her. At all." I glared at him. "I thought your judgment would've been better than that."

I didn't wait for a look or a response, just teetered toward the front door—the teetering might have taken away from any haughty edge I thought I had on him.

Inside the house, Mom glanced up from where she was caressing a blanket with a fuzzy lamb sewed on the front. She had an open box next to her.

Dear God, the presents had started coming.

She dabbed away some wetness from the corner of her eye. "It's late, pumpkin. Dinner's in the fridge."

I stood there and looked down at myself. I was covered in dirt, scratches, and blood. Not to mention I was drunk. Dinner's in the fridge? For real? Epic mom fail.

Landon peeked in from the kitchen. "You couldn't have got this girl into dance? Gymnastics? Even hockey would leave less battle scars. How's a girl like her ever going to get into college?"

Mom *hmmmed*, still off in her own world of blankies and lambs.

"Mattie's here," I announced. Mattie became very still behind me. He hated when I did that, but I hated when they ignored him. I felt Mattie's fist tap the small of my back. *Shut up!*

"Hello, Mattie," Mom said without looking back up from her presents.

Landon grunted, then clicked on the TV.

The listening-to-Cass portion of the evening was over. I wanted to scream at them, but what good would it do? Mattie pushed on me until I started moving toward the kitchen. I wasn't sure what my body should be doing next. I leaned against my elbows on the counter, my hands covering my face. When Mattie leaned in to check on me I grabbed him into a headlock and pressed my forehead into his temple. "I'm sorry." It wasn't just for embarrassing him in front of my parents, but also for being a bitch to him about Marilyn. But he knew what I meant.

Me too.

I wanted to tell him about Marilyn. About the fact that I was seeing Cooper and apparently so was she. But it would reveal more about me than about Marilyn. I wasn't ready for any revealing conversation with Mattie—of anything.

Just as he started to get an arm around me, I released

him and stepped away so we could grab snacks and tea bags.

Upstairs, in the hall outside my room, Henry looked up at us from his drawing notebook. He reached out his arm and waved his hand. "Hi, Cassie. Hi, Mattie." He even remembered to smile, though his eyes still resisted contact. Mattie returned the smile with an up-nod and gave Henry a fist bump as we walked by.

"Cass?" Henry whispered.

I squatted down. "Yeah, bud?"

"You got dirty." He brushed the top of my right hand with his fingertip.

"I know. I'm gonna clean up," I said.

"I like Mattie. He talks to me with his eyes. Does he talk to you like that?" Henry asked.

"Yeah, sometimes," I said.

"You have to open your heart to hear," Henry said.

I ran my hand over his hair. "Yeah. I guess so."

×

In my room I pulled out some track pants and a clean T-shirt from my dresser. Leaving Mattie flopped down on my bed with half of a granola bar in his mouth, I ducked out to the bathroom. Using a trick Mattie's mom taught me, I filled the sink, mixing cool water with chamomile and green tea bags. Healing properties or something. I crouched over the sink and soaked up to my elbows loosening the bits of sand and grit. I flexed my right hand, wincing at the sting of my knuckles from when I'd hit the tiled wall. The list lay next to me.

I dried my hands and found a nub of a pencil in the drawer. I wrote *fighting with Cooper* next to Devon's name, and *covering for me?* next to Eli's. It wasn't a reason why Eli would be guilty, but it was suspicious.

For no reason my mind wandered back to Mattie with Marilyn. Damn I really hated her.

I let out the plug and tossed the tea bags in the garbage under the sink. The sweet smell was lulling me into sleepiness. Well, that and the alcohol still buzzing through my brain. I'd been talking tough in the van, but I really did need to find someone at school to help me. I picked up my phone off the counter next to the sink and found the new contact. Brady. He could help me. I could let him, but the kissing stuff would have to be kiboshed. The thought of kissing him made me think of Cooper kissing me. Later. I would think about it all later. I showered quickly and redressed in my clean track pants and T-shirt. My fingers hovered over the keypad for a moment as I tried to think of something coherent and not at all needy to say.

Can we talk more?

His answer came back in seconds with a *ding*. **Yes?**

I texted him back and forth a few more times. He tried to get me to call him, but I put him off, the brief rush of reaching out to him wearing off, and the fatigue settling back in. **Tomorrow** I texted, dashing off my address and then belatedly wondering if Mattie would still be here and whether I wanted him with me when I talked to Brady.

Back in my room, I did a quick glance to Mattie in my bed watching *Cops*. Still waiting for one more return text from Brady, I reached for my hairbrush on the edge of my desk. The knock at my door made my hand twitch, and the brush did a double flip onto the rug.

"Gah! What?" I called out.

Mom opened the door and looked first at Mattie, then to me.

"The garbage can is still out on the street from this morning. That's your job. Don't forget—"

"I didn't forget!" I yelled. Of course I'd forgotten. Not like garbage pick-up schedules and chore lists were even on my radar at the moment. I pulled on my socks and sneakers. I stomped down the stairs and through the kitchen, stepped through the mudroom into the garage and hit the button for the big garage door. It creaked and protested as it did its work. I heard a dog bark.

I stomped down the driveway with heavy legs. Grabbing the handles of the garbage can, I tipped it toward me. I pulled it along, the plastic scraping against the concrete of the driveway. It wasn't until I reached the top, and the noise stopped with my movement, that

I realized how loud it had been. My ears pricked up at the silence. The dog had been brought in, along with the kids. The breeze rattled the leaves and I shivered. I jerked my head as a car went by. I was about to turn when I saw it: a shadow pulling out from the bushes, backlit by the streetlight on the corner.

I edged forward to get a better look and the shadow pulled back. I froze. *Hello?* I yelled in my head. But only a puff of air came out.

The breeze blew again and goose bumps erupted over my arms and legs and the fear started to tickle the back of my neck.

I dashed through the garage and hit the button, expecting someone would be ducking under the closing door to get me. But no one did. My heart was still pounding when I got back to my room.

Mattie hadn't bothered pulling back the covers. He was sleeping facing the wall and snoring. I climbed in next to him and lay on my back. I listened to the loud ticking of my wall clock. How had I ever slept with that sound? I rolled over and bent my knees until they touched Mattie, just barely. I felt my body relax as I exhaled, and sleep finally came.

Chapter 19

I was in the woods again. I looked down and wondered why I was always barefoot in these dreams. I didn't see any blood this time, so I started to walk. I could see them through the trees before I reached them. Cooper and Marilyn were sitting on a log. Our log. He started kissing her, both of his hands dug deep into her dark hair. Then he turned with a jerk toward me. Marilyn disappeared and Cooper reached his hand out to me. My own hand started to lift until I saw the blood leak through his hairline and into his face. I pulled my hand back.

"No," I whispered.

"Come here, Cass," he said in a calm voice, oblivious to the blood that was soaking his hair and running down the side of his face. I was backing up, or trying to, but my feet were sliding. I looked down and saw the mud as my feet sank deeper.

"Cassssssss." The hiss made me scream and I covered my ears.

He was reaching for me, hands on my shoulders. I twisted and turned to break his grip.

"No!"

I awoke and jumped out of bed, looking around my room to get my bearings. Mattie was gone. The pain shot through my head like a bullet and I clutched it with a groan. My mouth felt like I'd been force-fed cat litter.

My clock said 9:28 a.m. My brain registered two words: School and Fuck.

I ignored my head as I commanded my shaky legs to my dresser and found my last clean uniform. I had my shirt on and had the tights halfway up one leg. I froze. Brain waking up. It was Saturday. Idiot. I flopped back on my bed and smashed my face into my pillow.

There was a knock and my door opened. My mom said, "Cassie someone's . . . are you okay?"

Now she asked.

"I thought it was a school day," I said into my pillow.

"It's not," she said.

"Yeah."

"Someone's here. Brian? Or—"

"Brady? Brady's here?" I asked, pushing up from the

bed. The memories of reaching out to him last night were slowly surfacing through my achy, clouded brain.

Before she could answer I slithered off the bed and onto my feet. I whipped off my tights and let them fly across the room. Mom shook her head at me and went out the door as I found some jeans and pulled them on. I changed out of the blouse for a T-shirt from my closet.

I was halfway down the stairs when I turned back to find a school hoodie.

Downstairs, Brady was on the love seat, and Landon and my mom were on the couch. Beyond embarrassing.

Brady stood when he saw me on the steps. "Hey, Cassie, I was wondering if you want to—"

"Yeah, let's go." I went straight to the door. Brady followed behind and we had almost made a clean escape when I heard my mom.

"Cassie," Mom said.

I held the door so Brady could step out. Mom got her arm around me and steered me back into the house. "Excuse us a minute, Brady," she said.

"Mom!" I yelled as she shut the door in his face.

"Who is this boy? I didn't even know you were seeing anyone," she said.

"Mother, I'm going for a walk, or a drive, maybe get a bite to eat. We're not headed to Motel Six. We'll catch up on all the deets later," I said.

I walked out and closed the door in her face. It was mean, I'll admit. But I don't think parental concern should be a switch to flip on when you're feeling up to it.

"Hey," Brady called, jogging a few steps to keep up with my stride.

I stopped. "What?"

"Can I take the lead? I'm the one who came to pick you up," he said.

"Oh, yeah. What are we doing?"

"You'll see."

×

The Flame was six blocks away from my house on Snelling—two blocks north of St. B's. I'd been there as a kid, but had since stayed away. The all-night service and location made it a constant hangout for St. B's teens. There was a sign on the wall that read: MANAGER RESERVES RIGHT TO ENFORCE $3.00 MINIMUM PER PATRON.

I wiped my sweaty hands on my jeans and tried to breathe normally as I glanced around, remembering this was where Cooper was before he died—according to Eli and Devon, and confirmed by the receipt from the pile of items Cooper had on him the night he died. But of course I wasn't supposed to know that. "What are we doing here?"

"I'll show you," Brady said.

We got a booth by the window and ordered a couple of Cokes. Brady ordered an egg platter of some kind.

The waitress looked at me. "I'm not hungry," I said.

"Eggs are a great hangover cure," Brady said.

I glanced back down at the menu. "Ham and cheese omelet. Side of bacon. Crispy. And really, really big water," I held my hands out wide. "Like, a bucket."

She nodded and walked off toward a scraggly bearded man waving at her from another booth.

Brady leaned forward. "We all hang out here on weekends. This is where he was that night. Cooper."

I leaned forward, too. "Where? Which booth was he in?" I whispered.

He turned and pointed two booths down. "There. On the end. With Eli, Devon, and Devon's girl, Hailey."

I nodded and couldn't take my eyes off the booth.

"Did you know him very well? Cooper?" he asked.

"No." It seemed like I didn't know him at all. "Not exactly."

Waitress dropped off two waters. Mine, of course, not any bigger than Brady's.

"Why don't you think that skater kid killed him?" Brady asked.

I took a few gulps of my water. I was sober, and not in a hurry to give everything away to a guy I'd met a day ago.

"To be honest? Between what I heard on the news, and what I've heard about that Gav kid threatening Cooper, it seems foregone."

I picked up my fork and started poking the tines into the palm of my hand. "Then why are we here?"

He shrugged. "I'm not sure I can help you, but I told you I'd listen." He gave me the shy-eyes. "And I kind of have a crush on you." He grinned at me with that cute gap in his teeth.

I sighed. Great. But I felt myself relax. The waitress dropped off two more Cokes. I waited until she was out of earshot again before starting in. I knew I needed to give a little info to get a little info.

"I've known Gav forever. He's actually a friend of mine."

I waited for some kind of reaction, but Brady merely nodded for me to continue.

"His character isn't something I can convince you of. It's something you know in your gut about someone. You probably think he's some thug from Frogtown, but it's so not like that. He might have threatened to hurt Cooper, to protect me or one of our friends, but he's not going to follow someone and then . . . you know?"

"But what if they met up and then fought? That's not—what do they call it?—premeditated," he said as he reached for his water glass.

"Yeah, but the cop said Cooper was texted. That's what brought him to the school. Hey!" I yelled as a new thought popped into my brain.

Brady choked on his water. "What?"

"I had a thought. Gav couldn't have texted Cooper, or there'd be a record of that and the cops would be all over it."

"The cops told you he got a text?"

"Well, I sort of overheard the cops talking to Eli and Devon . . . while hiding nearby," I said.

"The cops don't know who the text was from?"

"Guess not. The cop had to ask Eli what it said."

"And Eli didn't know?"

I shook my head. "At least that's what he said."

"So they don't have Cooper's phone?"

I thought about that. It made sense. "Guess not, because why else would they be asking?"

"Right. If they had Cooper's phone they'd have the text and they'd have booked Gav the first night," Brady said.

"If it was from him." I shifted in my seat. "Which I don't think it was. I can't believe they charged him at all. Everything they have is weak. There was blood on his board from their fight in the park, and they don't even know for sure Gav was at the school that night."

"I heard about the fight. Were you there?" Brady asked.

I hesitated. "Yeah, but this all needs to stay with us. You get that, right?"

"I got that. Are you leading a double life, Cass?"

If only you knew. "I guess I am."

"Do you have any ideas? Any . . . alternative scenarios?"

I remembered Greta's revelation. "Did Cooper and Devon have some kind of fight?"

Brady looked around. "Between us, right?"

I nodded.

"There had been this tension between Devon and Cooper. Right at the beginning of the school year there was something going on with Cooper and Hailey, Devon's girl."

I swallowed. "What kind of something?" I asked, working hard to appear interested, but not in a I-just-had-a-mini-stroke kind of way.

"Like, hugging in the hall, sneaking into the peer counseling office together—"

"That doesn't mean anything."

"—and kissing."

I set my fork down. "When? When was there . . . kissing? And this is Devon's girlfriend?" This was it.

"Yeah. It was after school—after a student council meeting Devon missed."

I slouched back down. "So one kiss. That's not exactly a grand affair, Brady."

"Well, one public kiss. But where there's smoke in the hall . . . there's probably fire in the peer counseling office."

I made a face. "That's not like a real saying, is it?"

"No, I just made it up. Cooper had a rep when it came to girls. Lots of girls. And it seems to be true. Marilyn . . . Hailey . . ."

I nodded so he'd move on. I rubbed my temple where I was sure an aneurysm was about to burst. "Tell me more about Devon and Cooper's 'tension.'"

"That's all it really was. There wasn't any breakout brawls in the hall or anything. Cooper and Devon were just . . . on the outs for a few days." He shrugged. "And then they were on the ins. It was weird. Quiet. But like an electric current that went through the whole school. I don't know. Hailey is still with Devon; Cooper started up with Marilyn. So I guess it blew over."

And then it was back to Marilyn.

"Don't tell anyone I said that. Everyone knows, but no one talks about it. It's like taboo." His eyes flashed a hint of panic. "I don't think Devon would have a sense of humor if people started talking about it now. Especially to insinuate he had anything to do with . . ."

"Don't worry. There's no one for me to tell. Do you know if there's some kind of record they keep when someone goes to see a peer counselor?"

"Yeah, I think so. Why?"

"I don't know. Maybe there was a reason Hailey was seeing Cooper in the peer counseling office. Maybe he was actually, I don't know, peer counseling her?"

"What difference does that make?" he asked.

"I'm not sure if it makes a difference or not, but I think it's worth checking out. If I can find some evidence that points to whether it was one kiss or something . . . more . . . it makes a difference whether or not Devon would want to"—I looked around—"you know."

He shrugged. "I'm friends with Jenna Roberts, one of the other peer counselors. She's in my American History. I think she likes me." He smiled, then let his face slack into seriousness. "I'll talk to her tomorrow," he said.

This was big. This was helping. "I really appreciate this," I said.

×

Brady and I met up before lunch on Monday. "Apparently peer counselors are required to fill out a form outlining what they talk about. The forms are kept in a binder or folder of some kind and are looked over by the school psychologist in case there's mention of abuse or threats of violence that they would need to report," he said.

"They don't happen to leave the office unlocked when they aren't in there?" I asked.

"Doubt it."

There was nothing to it but to do it. "Okay. Do you think you can help me again?"

I stopped by the peer counseling office before going to class. There was a sign-up sheet on a clipboard hanging outside the door. Unfortunately, someone had cleaned out any previous days, so the only other sheets on the board were for new openings. So no quick check-to-see when Hailey had been here. I signed up in a time slot under Jenna's name for three o'clock—twenty minutes after my last class. If I could get in the office, I could find the notebook. Brady could provide some sort of distraction and—

Turning from the door I collided into a chest. I looked up. It was Eli. He steadied me with his hands, but left them tight on my upper arms. "I know who you are."

"What?" I said, wriggling under his hold.

"You're the skater girl who is friends with Gav."

I stilled.

He dropped his hands, but stayed in my space. "Why were you at Cooper's memorial party? Little early for Halloween costumes."

"Trying to figure out who killed Cooper," I said.

"You know who did it. He's your friend." He smiled. He actually smiled. "Any of this ringing a bell?"

"Oh, now we're teasing? Are you going to tell every-one? That I'm friends with him? Get me beat up maybe?"

He rolled his eyes. "Keep your head. If you want me to keep that a secret I'd cool it on the accusations crap."

"What is that? Are you offering to protect me? Why *wouldn't* you tell?" I said.

"Because I think I might know something else about you."

I stayed very still.

"And I haven't made up my mind about you."

I opened up my mouth to question him, to prod him maybe.

But he held up his hand. "I'm trying really hard not to hate you. You have to cool it with the sneaking around and talking to our friends."

"Gav didn't do it. I need to find out what happened," I said.

His eyes flashed. "You're pretty nerve-y. You go ahead and sneak around. Ask your questions." He leaned in to whisper in my ear. "But then don't walk home alone."

He bumped my shoulder for good measure and nearly toppled me over. Damn ballers. I was getting sick of being outrun and outmuscled by them.

×

I showed up for my three o'clock peer counselor appointment four minutes late and out of breath. I knocked on the door and a girl about my height with jet-black hair that hung in her face answered. She rocked her tight black jeans and had a wide smile that was more welcoming than her color palate.

"Come on in," she said.

The room was claustrophobic. It was a glorified closet with two chairs and a narrow table topped with a three-ring binder and a tissue box. A binder! Well, at least I wouldn't need to search. I plopped down and glanced around at the movie and band posters on the walls—all about five years old.

Jenna slid the binder out from under the tissue box and onto her lap. She started on about the confidentiality agreement they had and what would be kept secret and what would not. She opened the notebook to the first clean worksheet with blank lines and boxes printed on it. She scribbled in her name and mine at the top, then pointed to where I should sign.

"What should I put as the reason for visit?" she asked.

My mind was blank. If I didn't come up with something, Jenna would still have the binder in her hands when the "spontaneous and totally unplanned interruption" came. I didn't want to say "Cooper." It would have been fine—I'm sure people were saying it all week, but I didn't want to have my name down in that book with his.

"I'm having trouble . . adjusting to this school. I have trouble making friends," I said.

There. No arguing with that.

She nodded sympathetically and scribbled on the sheet.

That business done, Jenna tucked the folder back under the tissues and folded her hands.

"So what's up?" she asked. I glanced at the door, and back to Jenna. She hunched forward. "Why aren't you making friends?" she asked more gently. "What are you afraid of?"

At the mention of the word, fear itself flamed to life in my chest. I thought of the girls in fourth grade dissing me when I started skating with Mattie. I thought about my dad and his lie after lie before he left. I thought about my stepdad emotionally holding me at arm's length. And me holding Mom and everyone else at arm's length.

I opened my mouth. "I'm afraid . . . that when the

next person leaves with a piece of my heart . . . there won't be anything left."

We stared at each other in silence. She broke it by looking at the floor, regrouping. Maybe people didn't usually answer so directly? She opened her mouth and a knock sounded at the door. This threw her off even more. "Um . . ."

Brady poked his head in. "I'm sorry. I need to talk to you, Jenna."

Her head jerked. "Brady? I'm in a session."

"It's important. Urgent, really." He kept his eyes on her.

She was shaking her head. Maybe she wasn't as sweet on him as he thought, but she was blushing. So I burst into tears. I sniffed twice and grabbed a handful of tissues and shoved them over my dry eyes.

"Maybe . . . we could take a little break?" she said.

I nodded my head, keeping the tissues over my face. The door closed.

I let the tissues fall and immediately grabbed the binder, causing the tissue box to slide with it, until it landed on the floor.

I made one glance at the door, then dug right into the binder. Lucky for me the worksheets had not been cleaned out in a long time. A sticky tab had been stuck to a page about a third of the way back, maybe indicating when the psychologist has done her last read-through.

Also lucky for me, there were a ton of visits logged for the days right after Cooper's death, but only four or five a week, on average, in the weeks before he died. Not a lot to leaf through. Before I reached Hailey's entries, my fingers stalled on one made the day before Cooper died.

Marilyn. Reason for visit: Depression. Two days before that: Depression. Two days before that: Depression.

I flipped through to a week after school started and found Hailey. Reason for visit: Stress. Mother is in hospital again.

Whoa. That didn't sound like a crap line to get in and make out with your counselor. Not that "depression" couldn't be legit. But it was vague.

Cooper had jotted a note in the margin: "Ms. Baker — please reassign Hailey." Below that something had been erased. At the top, in loopy handwriting, it said, "Reassigned. Inappropriate attachment."

One visit before that: "Stress: Mom recently diagnosed with cancer."

Two visits before, Hailey is with Jenna, with a note—possibly to the psychologist: "Referring to Cooper. With his mom's history, he might be able to give her more specific advice with coping?"

Jenna opened the door, with her head still turned away I had about one second to slip the binder back on to the table.

"I need to get going," I said, standing, before she could say anything. "This has been really helpful." I took a step and felt something crunch under my shoe. I looked down and saw the crumpled tissue box. Reaching down, I handed it to Jenna. She narrowed her eyes. Her attention turned to the binder that was turned forty-five degrees from the position where she had set it down.

"What's going on?" she asked, pointing at the binder. The welcoming smile was gone.

"I wanted to read that agreement a little more closely." I started to move toward the door.

She stared me down. "I saw you."

My stomach fell. I didn't say anything.

"I saw you one day by the loading dock door with Cooper." She sat down and tears filled her eyes. "He was a sincerely nice guy. A lot better at this than I am."

Jenna didn't seem mad, or like she was about to call security on me, so I sat back down.

She continued. "Did you care about him?"

"Yes," I said.

She nodded and rubbed her hands on her jeans. "Good. I never liked Marilyn. Coming here all the time, sniffing after Cooper."

"You don't think she had real problems?" I said.

"Oh, that girl has a truckload of real problems. But I don't think that's why she ever came here."

"Was she really dating him?"

"I wish I could tell you no, but I don't know," Jenna said. "We didn't talk about personal stuff like that."

"What about Hailey?"

Jenna looked a little surprised. "No. I know for sure and I'm not spilling that as her peer counselor. I'm sharing it as her friend who doesn't want her to get a rep for rumors of something that never happened. It was just that one kiss." She winced. "Poor girl. Sadness can get emotions all confused."

I nodded.

"You want to know anything else about Cooper, you ask. You don't have to snoop around, okay?"

"Okay," I said.

"And if you want to talk more about making friends, and being afraid? I'm here for that, too," she said.

She opened up her arms and I let her hug me.

"You are good at this," I told her. And I meant it.

×

I caught Brady up on the drive back to my house.

"So you don't think Cooper and Hailey had a thing?" Brady said.

"I don't know. Hailey was seriously needing counseling—it wasn't just an excuse to see Cooper. She didn't even start with Cooper as her counselor," I said. "Is this a bootleg? I have all of Geotrash's songs, but I've never heard of this one."

Brady glanced down. "Buddy of mine recorded it at their '09 concert at First Avenue. But Cooper and

Hailey did kiss," he said. "That was a witnessed event."

I selected the Geotrash song called "Recycled Love" and let it play out through the first verse and back into the chorus—tapping the beat out with my thumb on the armrest—before answering. "Yes. But for all we know that was the only time. That's what Jenna said, too. Cooper asked for Hailey to go back to Jenna after that. The school psychologist called it 'inappropriate bonding,' or attachment or something. I think Hailey just got confused."

"So you don't think Devon killed Cooper?" he asked.

I shook my head. "I can't rule him out completely. He's still on the list. He doesn't exactly strike me as someone who would take something like that with a cool head."

"Yeah. I'd run with that. He's got a temper all right. I've seen it," he said.

"Right. But I don't know why he'd wait two weeks to do it." I shrugged. "For now he stays on the list. And so does Eli."

"Why is Eli on there?" he asked as he turned onto my street.

"I . . . bumped into him today and he was a bit . . . hostile. He knows I'm friends with Gav—that I'm the skater girl who was at the fight at the park." I couldn't exactly tell Brady that Eli might know about me and Cooper . . . because Brady didn't know about me and

Cooper. I shouldn't have lied about that. But I'd lied to everyone else already. Why would I have told him the truth five seconds after meeting him? "He knows we were at the memorial party and that I'm looking into stuff. He didn't seem to appreciate that."

Brady pulled into my driveway and shifted into park. He adjusted his glasses. "Do you want me to pick you up in the morning?"

I sighed as I unhooked my seat belt. "I don't want to be babysat."

Brady shifted in his seat. "Look. I get that you were drunk the other night and you have a lot on your plate right now. I don't know how all this is going to work out, but it seems to me like you might need a friend."

He said the word "friend" carefully and deliberately. I appreciated when people were deliberate with their words, and that he seemed to get the whole kissing thing was shelved. "Okay. You can pick me up . . . friend," I said, not sounding obvious at all.

After dinner, I did about a half hour of math before getting a restless head. I couldn't concentrate. Mattie had been absent from my life for two days. I looked around my room like he might be there. But he was missing. And I felt it. I checked my phone again. He hadn't texted. But neither had I.

Was he okay? Was he hooking up with Marilyn? I had no right to be fussed about that—except that she may or may not be involved in Cooper's death. So in a way I had every right to keep her far from Mattie, even if he thinks he's investigating.

But it wasn't that. I missed him. Without giving it another thought I stood from my desk. I needed to see him.

My skateboard was sitting on the mat by the back door. It felt like years since I had properly been out on it. I missed it. But the missing-it feeling was wrapped up with missing the boys. I picked it up. Just having my hands on the board felt better already. Stepping outside, I considered going back up to my room for my iPod, but thought maybe it was better to keep my listening ears on. I pulled the door tight and locked it.

Did I really think that Eli and/or Devon and/or anyone else would come after me? It was all fine and good in the light of day, but the thought was making me nervous in the dark. I texted Mattie.

I m coming ovr

I prayed Marilyn wasn't there.

I pushed myself as soon as I hit the pavement. Riding fast helped with the fear-soaked adrenaline. Even though I usually associated skating with the boys, there was still something therapeutic and inherently me in the movement. It surprised me how much my body missed it. But the paranoia kept creeping in.

I kept on the main drags. Up Snelling, down University, then up Rice to Mattie's street, which was dark and quiet compared to the bright lights and traffic. The whir of my wheels was loud in my ears. I straightened my right leg, grinding the back of the board down to a sliding stop. Stepping off, I popped my board up to carry it the rest of the way.

When I was two houses away from Mattie's, I looked back toward Rice. That's when I felt hands gripping my shoulders. I heard my board hit the pavement. My breathing stopped and every cell in my body flinched as I spun back, ready to fight.

Mattie.

I punched him, anyway—hard, in the chest. I relaxed half an inch, but the adrenaline had already brought tears to my eyes. He was smiling as he rubbed the place where I'd hit him, until he saw how upset I was.

Reeling me into him, he wrapped his long arms around me. I listened to his heartbeat as I held on to him at his waist with both hands. The tears ran freely down my face, and I let them soak his shirt. My body shook against him as I tried to breathe.

It's okay. I'm sorry. Shhhhhh.

He ran a hand over the crown of my head, then landed a kiss there, causing a ripple of chills to run down my spine. The good kind. The emotion welled up so fast it was all I could do to choke back more tears.

Mattie let go and tried to pry off my grip, but I wasn't ready to let go. He reached up and cradled my face in his hands, but I kept my eyes pinched shut and tried to twist away. I couldn't look at him. I didn't want to look at his face . . . and fall in love with it even more.

I broke away just to have him get ahold of me again. This time he let my head burrow into him. And he just held me. Too long. Breaking all my rules that I set for our own safety. But safety was becoming a relative term. The idea of safe emotions was becoming a blurry concept. My need to feel safe in every other way overwhelmed me.

I stepped back because I had to, and he let me.

"You scared me," I said. Picking up my board, I walked away from him toward his house before he could answer. "I hope you're gonna feed me, because I could eat a cow's hide through fence slats."

Mattie found my hand in the dark and laced his fingers in mine, but he didn't say anything.

He led me in and we watched two hours of I-don't-even-know-what and ate cold leftovers of it-didn't-matter. Stretched out on the couch with my pillow on Mattie's leg, and the weight of his arm around my waist, it didn't matter. Just being there with him did.

Mattie's mom woke me at I don't even know what time. Mattie's hair stood up all over, not just his cowlick. I listened to the rumble of his soft snore. I didn't want to leave. The ache in my chest had returned, and I hadn't even left him yet. Mattie's mom looked tired, still in her navy blue nurse scrubs. She tugged my hand. "Come on, Cass. I'll give you a ride home."

×

The next morning I felt like shit. I must have looked it, because Landon actually offered me a ride to school. Though, I bet I didn't lower the awkward factor at all when I spent the silent ride with my forehead pressed against the cool glass of the window. I felt Landon's worried eyes on me.

First period. I was still half asleep. It wasn't until the tie was in my face (peaches this time) that I realized he was there.

"Hello, Cassie," Limey said.

I offered him a sunshiny smile. "Great to see you, but you're standing between me and a tardy slip in Sister Rita's class."

"I doubt that will be a problem. Me and the Sister? We're like this," Limey said.

I doubted the Sister was "like that" with anyone . . . hence being a Sister. But I took his meaning. Sister Rita was the only other one who knew about Cooper and me, and maybe she'd ratted me out. Governed by honesty? Either that or Eli.

I could feel the stares and whispers all around me. The bell rang overhead, but the hall was still crowded and no one was moving.

"Is there somewhere we can go? Buy me a caramel latte? Haul me off downtown for questioning?" I asked in a low voice.

Limey just crossed his arms. "Naw. You seem to lie when we're out together. Maybe here you'd tell the truth about what I found out."

He was going to say it. He was going to out me in front of everyone.

My mouth was dry. "Who needs books, right?" I started to turn away.

I heard him bang the locker. "Is this one Cooper's? And this one yours?" Another bang. "How cute. Pretty convenient for slipping in love letters back and forth."

I forgot how to breathe. I was aware of every sound around me. Someone gasped, and there was a soft "oh," but otherwise silence.

I turned back. I could lie. I could rail on him, but . . . I felt like a fever was creeping up my neck.

"Why didn't you tell me you guys were seeing each other?" He stepped away from the lockers toward me. "Phone records show quite a lot of texts between you two. Wonder what they said?"

I glanced around.

What Cooper and I had together was mine. Was. Now I wondered how it would be twisted into something ugly, something . . . other.

I bolted. Not in a resisting arrest kind of way, but

in protest of how I wouldn't let this cop dictate how this would go down. I took the stairs two at a time and pushed through the outside door.

Limey was barely out behind me, finding me when I layed into him.

"You had no right to out me in front of everyone," I said.

"I think I did. You lied to me about your relationship with Cooper."

"So you teach me a lesson through public humiliation? This is high school. It would have been kinder to take me out and stone me."

I felt the tear slip and scratched it from my cheek. His look softened and I hated what he must be thinking.

"Sorry," he said with a shrug.

"Save it. You're not. And neither am I. Gav couldn't give two shits who I dated. It had nothing to do with anything, so I didn't feel it was any of your business. Still don't."

"It is my business. You lied. I had your phone records pulled. That's how investigations work," he said.

"And I bet you pulled Gav's phone records, too. So you know he didn't text Cooper."

"The text was from a prepay. It could have been anyone. How did you know about the text?" he asked.

"I only know there was one. It's all around school." I shifted my weight. "Too bad you don't have Cooper's phone because then you'd know what it said."

He gave me a long look. "We found pieces of it on the path, but I don't need the phone or the text. I think what you need is to consider the possibility that Gav did it. There's a good chance it was in the moment. Something set him off . . ."

I took a deep breath. "You're wrong." I had to give him something. "Maybe there's another reason he could have been killed." I took the list from my pocket and held it out to him. He glanced at it but didn't take it. "What if Cooper found out about some dealing at school? There'd be a chance someone buying was pissed about him getting involved."

"Involved how?"

I opened my mouth and stalled.

"Cassie? How did he get involved? Who's the dealer?" he asked.

He was stepping in on me and I had nowhere to go.

"What you have to understand is that it wasn't the dealer who got killed, it was Cooper. So if you take Gav out of the equation . . ."

"Gav? Gav is the dealer?" He laughed. "I see how I was wrong about sweet old Gav."

I ignored him. "It's still a possible solution that this has something to do with the drug-dealing situation, but not Gav. And then there's Devon who—"

"We are not investigating this murder together. Besides, I think I have everything I need. You will be called to testify."

He smoothed down his fruity tie and walked away, leaving me still holding out the list like an idiot. Shit all. I kicked the wall next to the school door to see if it would make me feel any better. It didn't.

The door next to me creaked open and Eli walked through.

I crossed my arms in front of me. "Eavesdrop much?"

He waited, stepping closer.

I eased back until my back was against the wall.

"I don't have to. I knew about Gav being a dealer, obviously. And I had my suspicions about you being the girl Coop was seeing. Then again, I didn't know you were going to tell a cop that Devon of all people is on your radar."

I didn't have a response prepared for that one.

"Why are you doing this?"

I thought about telling him how much I cared about Gav, how he was like a brother. But there was another reason I thought he could relate to more. "I want to find out who did it. I cared about Cooper, too."

He narrowed his eyes. "Did you? Care about Cooper? I don't know that. I don't know you. You show up at our memorial party like it's a joke; sneak around the peer counseling office snooping on Hailey—yes, I did hear about that—and now you're telling a cop that my best friend had reason to kill my other best friend. Really? It's all because you cared about Cooper? Listen to me:

people are gonna know about you and Cooper now, and Devon can add two and two. If you don't want to get hurt, you and your friends should steer clear. Next skater who even sets foot at St. B's or one of our parties again is going down. You better make yourself small."

Chapter 20

I somehow made my way through the day on autopilot. Like sometimes in the car, when you get so wrapped up in a thought, and when you get to where you're going you can't remember the ride. I ignored the whispers. Which was easy—I was used to not paying attention to people at this school. Faces and voices were a blur.

I wasn't scared, though maybe I should've been. I was confused. Was Eli helping me? How does a guy use threats and still make it seem like he's helping?

At the end of the day, Brady was at his locker. He didn't smile at me as I approached.

"Why are you looking at me like that?" I said, trying to play it cool, even though he must have heard about me and Cooper. "Just ask me," I said.

"You were seeing Cooper." He waited. For what, I wasn't sure. So I waited, too.

"You have anything you want to say about that?" he said.

"No. What do you want me to say? We were seeing each other, okay? I'm sorry I didn't tell you." I rubbed the sweat from my palm onto my skirt. "You still helping me?"

He sighed. "I said I would. *I* didn't lie."

I glanced around and stepped closer. "I didn't exactly lie. You asked me if I knew him well. Lately I've been thinking I didn't know him at all. We were seeing each other for two weeks, during which I broke up with him twice."

He looked at me. "While he dated Marilyn."

Ouch.

"Did you know about Marilyn?" he said.

"No. I wouldn't date around with him behind some chick's back. I thought it was just me."

He slouched against his locker. "I hate when girls lie."

"I don't like it when anyone lies." I punched his arm, in what I hoped was a consoling way. "I'm sorry. Really."

His eyes darted over my right shoulder.

"Hey," he said.

I turned as a hulk of a guy rolled by. Shaved head. Gobbers. He high-fived Brady's waiting hand and went into the guy's bathroom. Gobbers was still on the list.

Brady still wasn't looking at me. I stepped in close and lowered my voice. "There's something else. Cooper told me Gav was dealing pot at St. B's. I didn't believe it at first—it was one of the reasons we broke up—but I talked with my friends and now we think it's true. I didn't say anything to you about it because I didn't want you to think bad of Gav."

Brady waved his hand. "Cass, it's okay. Just tell me."

"Okay. I want to figure out who he was selling to. I'm thinking if Gav was selling drugs, Cooper might have tried to stop him with that whole peer-leader thing he had going. And maybe that wouldn't sit too well with Gav's buyers."

"Who was he selling to?"

"I don't know for sure. We saw Gav with Marilyn here at St. B's, and Cooper told me she said Gav was 'pushing' it on her—whatever that means—and I saw Gav once with your friend, Gobbers."

Brady dipped his head. "You saw Gobbers buying drugs?"

Crap. I'd just inadvertently accused one of Brady's friends of doing drugs, and possibly having something to do with a murder. "No, I just saw them talking. Sorry. It's just somewhere to start. Was he at the Flame that night?"

Brady thought for a sec. "Gobbers was. But not for very long. I don't think Marilyn was there at all that night."

"Do you think he'd talk to me? Gobbers? Maybe he knows something?"

"If you're with me, he'll talk. We're cool like that," he said.

I took a step toward the boy's bathroom where he'd yet to emerge from. Brady pulled me back with a laugh. "No, not like that! Later, later."

"So you're still helping me?"

He rolled his eyes. "Yes, Cass. Correct me if I'm way off here, but it seems like you have this thing. Like you're expecting people to hurt you? Like a trust thing? And I get that. I do. But you're becoming so good at pushing people away, that unless you find someone to pull *in*, the result is going to be the same."

I was saved from having to respond when I saw his gaze was drifting over my shoulder again. Two girls were standing in front of a locker quietly brushing away tears.

"What?" I asked him.

"Do you think those girls are really upset, or is it just a play for attention?" he said.

I shrugged. "Upset for real."

"Really?"

I looked over again. One of them was wearing a letter jacket with a tennis racket patch and her grad year—this spring. "Yeah, well, if they're seniors, the girls probably knew him. So I guess they're for real."

"Really?"

"Why do you keep saying that? I thought everyone loved Cooper."

"I liked Cooper, and I know it's not cool to talk about someone who is dead, but sometimes I questioned his character. Maybe he wasn't as much of a leader as we thought he was."

"What do you mean?"

"You know. The way he dated around. Even hitting on his best friend's girl? Cheating on Marilyn. I would think it'd make a lot of girls hate him, so it surprises me, I guess, they'd be so upset."

"What about the guys? Has Gobbers been upset about his friend?"

Brady tipped his head to the side and narrowed his eyes. "I was Cooper's friend, too, but I don't cry every day. So what? Everyone deals differently."

"I'm sorry. I'm just trying to figure out how everyone fits together. Everyone has to be fair game in theory."

Brady shut his locker. "Gobbers and I were tight with Cooper. I really don't think he has any reason to hurt him."

"You were tight with Cooper? Really?" I never saw Cooper say two words to him, and the same for Devon or Eli.

He shrugged. "Not tight, but we've grown up together. Same private schools since kindergarten. Everybody likes us, and I've never heard about Gobbers having any beef with Cooper. I'd know."

"Okay, but I have to ask him about Gav," I said.

"Later, okay? I'll take you to his house."

×

As we stepped out the front entrance after school, my "attention radar" was going off. There was a lot of staring going on in my direction. One of two girls on the steps broke off midsentence to run her eyes over me. Tight groups of kids were hanging in front of the school. The talking all but stopped as they turned toward me. Some of them kept on with their behind-their-hand whispers and barely concealed pointing. At the bottom of the stairs Devon had his arm slung around the crying blonde from the party. I assumed she must be his girlfriend, Hailey. She whispered in his ear. She was pretty, but not steely perfect like popular girls in movies. She looked mousy small, her strawberry-blonde hair thin, but shiny.

Probably thanks to social media, apparently everyone knew about me and Cooper. When we reached the bottom of the stairs, Devon stepped in on me and pointed in my face. "I know who you are," he said, loud enough for everyone to hear. "I know you were seeing Coop."

"She's cool, Devon," Brady said.

"She's not fucking cool! She and her friends killed Coop!"

He knew. I guessed Eli was right about Devon being able to add two and two. I wasn't just the girl who went out with Cooper, I was the skater girl who was with Gav at the park. A murmur ran through the crowd. They all seemed to take two steps closer. Including half the football team.

Brady took his arm back, his shoulder rolling in front of mine, so he was half shielding me. "Dial it back, dude. She didn't have anything to do with that."

Brady was wiry solid, with at least three inches on Devon, but Devon was above average height and also thick, as were the ballers closing ranks. This could get ugly.

Devon kept his scowl on me, ignoring Brady. "You make me sick. Showing up to Cooper's memorial like it's some kind of joke."

"I'm not laughing about his death, and nothing about dating him was a joke," I said.

"Until all your boyfriends got involved."

The anger bubbled in my stomach. "Well, you'd be the expert on love triangles with Cooper."

There was a stunned silence. I had breached the taboo. Even Brady glanced back, like he couldn't believe I had the balls. Hailey's whole face was one big, tiny pinch.

Devon moved closer to Brady and me, but his eyes were on me. Eyes that looked like he could kill me. The whole crowd took another step in.

Through the nervous twittering of the crowd, I heard the wheels and slapping of boards. Devon turned his head toward the sound as everyone shifted their attention toward the street, where Mattie and Franklin were rolling up. Mattie leaned against the rail of the fence searching everyone's faces for mine. Franklin, the dick, was smiling.

"Hey, bitches!" Franklin said with a wave.

Devon started to move toward them and a wave of movement ran through the footballers as they shifted to follow, like a pack of zombies smelling brain meat. Eli stepped in front of Devon blocking him. "Cool it, Dev. The cops got the guy. The others aren't worth missing the Homecoming game for, right?"

Devon glanced back at me, then over my shoulder.

I looked back. Headmaster Spanders was perched at the top of the stairs. Devon seemed unsure for a sec, then heaved out a breath. "Right, Eli. Friday is for Cooper." He lowered his voice. "But if I get a chance with one of those fuckers, they are dead." He bit out the last word in my face.

He pulled Hailey along with him toward the parking lot and I chuffed out a breath. When I looked up, Eli was watching me. He'd defended me again. First at the party, then to the cop. And now in front of Devon.

I watched the rest of the ballers walk past Mattie and Franklin. One of them spit on Franklin's Converse.

"You owe me thirty bucks, bitch," Franklin yelled after the guy.

"Franklin, shut up," I said quietly as I gave his shoulder a shove. "What the hell are you doing here? I thought we agreed to meet later."

"We were coming this way anyway and I like riling the assholes." He looked at Brady. "Who are you?"

"I'm helping Cass," Brady said, in a steady enough voice, but he looked supremely uncomfortable.

"Why?" Franklin said.

"Stop," I whispered to him, even though Brady could obviously hear. "Not everyone at this school is an asshole."

When the moment broke with a bored sigh from Franklin, I noticed he was wearing what looked like a sheet tied at his waist over his jeans. He had to be freezing with nothing but a short-sleeved white T-shirt under it.

"What are you wearing?" I said.

"Toga."

"I wasn't aware they were starting a new dress code at Kellogg," I said.

"It's Spirit Week. Homecoming is Friday. Same as you guys," Franklin said.

"And you were moved by the spirit?"

"Eh. I just like togas," Franklin said.

I looked at Mattie. "Brady is taking me to see that guy I saw with Gav. Can we catch you guys later? My house in a couple hours?"

Mattie didn't answer.

"Is that okay with you?" I asked a little more sharply.

Brady leaned toward me. "Does he even talk?"

"Do what you gotta do," Franklin said, answering for Mattie. "We're getting some eats with the girls."

The girls? The plural confused me, but I let it go.

When they'd rode off, Mattie texting, I turned to Brady. "As pissed as I get about people assuming we're no good because of the neighborhood we come from, I'm painfully aware the prejudice goes both ways. I'm sorry."

"It's okay."

"It's not. I appreciate we're friends. Even if it started out weird. And I don't want you to think I'm using you."

"I don't think that. And I don't blame you for having trust issues with this school. Cooper manipulated you."

I silently digested the comment. I thought of Cooper's smiles and lines. Well practiced. He'd probably played the game countless times before. But the thing was, it never felt that way. I can usually smell a player a mile away. It never felt like he'd been holding back or overcompensating.

"You still want to talk to Gobbers?" Brady said, interrupting my thoughts.

"Yeah. Devon is sliding right into prime suspect position in my mind, but he could just have serious anger management issues. Wouldn't be the first athlete. We should keep getting info on the drug angle."

"Don't take this wrong, but do your friends have alibis?" he said as we walked.

I stopped. "What?"

"I could be wrong, but I'm sensing some anger on their end, too." He flashed me a wincing smile to soften the blow. "Just keeping it real, you know, since my friends are all fair game."

A flame of fear licked at my insides. I couldn't start suspecting my friends. Not without going insane. But he had a point. He'd been more than cool about me flinging near-accusations at his group, so I couldn't fault him for bringing up mine.

"Franklin doesn't have anger issues, exactly. He just has . . . issues."

Brady nodded for me to continue.

"He has insecurities. I guess insecurities that we all have. We've met enough popular people, or people with money, or popular people with money who look down on us. You start to assume they're all like that. He's been jumped more than once." I swallowed and thought about it some more. "Gav and Mattie, too. As a girl I don't get beat on like they have, though I've had plenty of shit talked to me. It's just made him hard, I guess. Maybe it's just confirmed things he's already thought? I don't know."

"It's easy on both sides to isolate ourselves with what we know—what's comfortable. It's easy to hate. We all do it and it's stupid to pretend we don't. There has to be a hell for there to be a heaven. There has to be hate in our heart for there to be love. You know? There has to be dark for there to be light. I don't blame them for hating Cooper."

"That's a lot of depressing shit, Brady."

He gave me a placating smile. "So . . . do they have alibis?" he asked.

"Franklin and I were at Mattie's—movie night—but Franklin left early to hook up with Greta, Gav's sister," I said.

"So, not a very tight alibi?"

"Well, I don't know. They're each other's alibis," I said. "It's tight."

"And the other? The quiet one?" He said it softly, but it felt like he had shouted. I didn't want to talk with him about Mattie. Especially about anything that would potentially crack the tight veneer of trust I had with him. Mattie was mine. He was probably the number-one reason I hadn't become a hard bastard like Franklin. Franklin didn't have a Mattie. I mean, he had Mattie, but not like I had Mattie.

"He was . . . we all fell asleep in Mattie's living room. When I woke up he was still on the couch. . . ." *with me*, I added to myself.

"He couldn't have left while you were sleeping?"

I thought about how he often left from my own bed without waking me. I clamped down on the thought. Mattie would never be on the suspect list, and now wasn't a good time to be thinking about him in my bed. "Cassie?"

"No," I said to Brady, though I'm sure he noticed the blush on my face. "It wasn't Mattie. Mattie's off-limits."

He didn't say anything, but he looked like he wanted to.

"It wasn't him," I said again.

He nodded, but I could tell he was pacifying me. "Okay. If you're sure. But you do realize they both have motives, right? With all the Cooper hating?"

I nodded. What else could I say?

×

Gobbers's house was only a block away from school, so we hoofed it. His house was big, not like Cooper's, but a really nice old A-frame like Landon's. Though the lawn looked like it was a week behind on the mowing compared to the next-door neighbor's, and the leaves hadn't been raked. Not out-of-control abandoned-looking, but just not as polished.

"My man!" Brady said with a smile after Gobbers opened the door.

Gobbers smiled with those teeth that were really unfortunate, but he had a sparkle to his blue eyes I hadn't noticed before. It made him kinda cute.

"What's up?" he asked us.

"We're on a tour of the neighborhood. You're a starred attraction," Brady said.

"Sweet."

Brady furrowed his brow. "Um, you gonna invite us in, bro?"

Gobbers's cheeks colored. "Um. Sure. Yeah, yeah. Come on."

I steeled myself as I went over in my head why we were here. It wasn't a social call. As cool as Gobbers seemed, I had to be on guard. Thankfully, I wasn't getting any I'm-going-to-kill-you-right-now vibe from him, and somehow I doubted he was going to get all Blair Witch on me with Brady right there. Nevertheless, as much as I downplayed for Brady, the fact that Gobbers knew Cooper and had something going on with Marilyn was plunking him right in my scope of suspects. Not to mention the shifty vibe he'd been giving me all week. Two questions remained: Did he have a motive, and did he have an alibi? Granted these were very large questions. I glanced around the yard before going up the steps after Brady.

The front room was dim as we walked in. Thick curtains were pulled tight over the windows. The room looked more like a hunting cabin than a typical living room. There were at least five different horned animal heads mounted on the walls. Also mounted were two pictures. One was a group of guys in camo, standing in the desert. Soldiers. The other was a group of firemen in front of a truck. One of them was on his knees, giving the camera the middle finger. His smile full of mismatched teeth looked just like Gobbers.

"Get away from there!" A gruff voice came from behind me.

Jerking away from the photo, I whipped around and

realized there was a man in a recliner on the far side of the room. He was struggling to stand.

"Sorry," I said, edging sideways until I bumped into Gobbers.

"Sorry, sir. Going downstairs now," Gobbers said. He grabbed my arm and pulled me along. Brady followed behind. In the kitchen there was some kind of sausage cooking on the stove, but no one watching it. We were descending the stairs to what I could only assume was Gobbers's basement bedroom, as I hoped we weren't going to become some kind of sausage.

Gobbers's room wasn't at all what I expected. Given his dad's taste, I expected some father/son similarity. There was zero camo. Zero indication that hunting was some kind of family deal. I didn't see any girly posters or car posters or girlies-on-cars posters, which I'd somehow expected was a given for his type. I almost missed it, but there was one picture of Gobbers with the St. B's football team, though no other school pride or jock theme going on. In fact, there didn't seem to be much theme at all. The room was simple, spotless, and nondescript. A tightly made bed sat in the corner with a spotless desk next to it. I had no basis of study, but to me this was classic serial-killer habitat—minus the trophies from his kills.

I nearly turned right around and would have left, if it wasn't for Brady's elbow—which woke me from my staring with a poke to my arm. We plopped down on the plain couch. Brady made some quick intros. "This is Cassie. Cassie, Gobbers."

Gobbers nodded but looked anywhere other than at me. He lowered himself into the matching black chair to our left.

"So, what's up?" he said.

I realized when he glanced down at my hands I was crackling my knuckles, so I tucked them under my knees. I could've spent time with getting-to-know-you pleasantries, but I'm all for ripping off the Band-Aid when it comes to awkward talk.

"I saw you with my friend Gav a couple weeks ago," I told him.

Gobbers looked at Brady. "He's the one they arrested?"

"Yeah," I answered before Brady. "I saw you guys out back after school. It was raining."

He smiled and his eyes went to Brady again. He rubbed his hands together. "What's this about, man?"

"Cassie doesn't think that skater guy killed Cooper. We're just poking around," Brady said with a shrug.

"Oh? Well, I didn't do it," Gobbers said. He let out a loud belly laugh that made me jump, then he dropped it as quickly as it started. This dude was either nervous or just plain odd.

"This is going to come out kind of whack, but I think we should cut right to it. Were you buying drugs from

Gav?" I asked.

He was nodding, but it was a continuation of the nod he'd started before I asked the question. His eyes were doing that far-off, spacey thing. I thought maybe he hadn't heard. I was about to ask again when he let out a short "No."

He smoothed a hand over his stubbly hair. "Not buying drugs from Gav . . . no. That would be a negative."

"Did you know he was selling?" I said.

Looking at the carpet he answered, "I may have overheard that."

"Come on, man. Overheard? Like in a radio ad? Gobbers, who was he selling to?" Brady pressed. "We're not going to get you kicked off the team."

I hadn't thought of that. Buying would definitely be a secret he'd want to keep.

Gobbers steepled his fingers and ran his pointers along the bridge of his nose.

He stared at Brady for what felt like a long time. And Brady was staring back. Brady leaned in farther toward Gobbers and narrowed his eyes. "Who was buying? Or who were you buying for?"

Gobbers hesitated and I jumped in with a follow-up.

"Cooper said that Gav was pushing on Marilyn, which doesn't really sit right with me," I said. "I've seen you with her, too. Do you know what the deal is with that?"

Another glance to Brady and then back to me. "No deal. I don't know about any deals. Just know her from around."

"Was she buying from Gav?"

Gobbers didn't reply. He was looking me over real good. Formulating, maybe. He broke the staring contest with a smile. "Here's the deal. I saw the skater kid doing tricks outside school and we got to talking. We started talking about partying and stuff. I mentioned how hard it was to get anything around here and know it's clean. A guy like me can't exactly be walking down University Ave. and buying off some homeless guy or gangbanger. The kid—Gav—said he could get me some. So, yeah."

He stopped so abruptly I thought he was just catching his breath, but apparently that was the end of his story, and also the end of our questioning. Gobbers stood up.

"You know of anyone else buying?" I asked.

Gobbers shot me a look. "No." There was a firmness to his voice. "Brady man, leave me off the 'tour' next time, yeah?"

"Sorry," Brady said.

But I wasn't ready to let it go. "What about Marilyn?"

"I'm no narc." His smile took on a chilly edge. "You want to know about Marilyn? You ask Marilyn." He walked toward the stairs, and we didn't have much choice but to follow. Before we were shuffled out the back door, I stopped. Gobbers was holding the door open.

"What time did you leave the Flame that night Cooper died?" I said.

"I don't know. Early. I wasn't feeling good," Gobbers said.

"Where'd you go?"

As he opened his mouth, his mom appeared behind him. "He came home. Alone." Her voice was low and croaky, like she was just getting over a cold. "I don't sleep well when Howard's on duty at the firehouse." She tipped her head to look at Gobbers who was staring a hole into the rug. "You going to invite your friends to stay for dinner, Jesse?"

Gobbers jerked his head up, but his eyes didn't meet hers. "No, Mom." he said. Brady and I moved past him as his mom disappeared back into the kitchen. Gobbers leaned onto the doorjamb. "I do hope you find out who did it. I'm sorry I couldn't help more."

I watched as emotion swam behind his eyes. Compassion? Guilt? Something real.

I leaned in, the emotion spiking in me, too. If he knew, if he fucking knew—"If you're hiding something—*anything?*—I need you to tell me. I could try to keep your name out of it, because I know they're your friends, but Gav—" My voice cracked on his name, but Gobbers was cutting me off anyway.

"We got a wild one here, Brady." Whatever I had seen in his eyes was gone and his goofy smile reemerged, but with a menace that hadn't been there before.

Brady pulled at my hand. "Sorry, dude," he said to Gobbers.

Gobbers went on, his whispered words sending spiking chills down my neck. "Nobody likes all that crazy talk around here, girl. The only thing I'm 'hiding' is that I bought from that guy, Gav. For obvious reasons. You gotta pipe down on all that accusing shit. That crazy talk gets people riled."

Gobbers fist-bumped Brady. After the door clicked shut behind Gobbers, I looked at Brady.

"Hey," I said. "Thanks for backing me up."

Brady didn't say anything.

"What was that all about?" I said. "He knows something and he was practically threatening me."

"He wasn't threatening you. Holding back? Yeah. And I don't know what that's all about, but he wouldn't threaten you. It's just truth. You keep on pushing people, they're gonna push back."

He looked like he was going to say something else, but he left it as a shrug before turning down the path to the sidewalk. I jogged to keep up with his long stride.

"Do you think he was buying for someone?" I said.

"Maybe. Maybe he was . . . protecting someone."

"Someone, who?"

Brady pushed up the bridge of his glasses. "I don't know for sure," he said. For sure? Was Brady holding out, too? To pay me back for withholding? I shook off the doubt and followed him down the driveway. I decided to let it go for now.

Trust. I had to start somewhere.

Chapter 21

I was starving, so there was no way I was going to pass up Brady's offer to "throw together a bite" at his house. The sky was giving us only a sliver of purple on the horizon, and the streetlights had all blinked on, so it felt later than it was.

Brady lived on the west side of Highland Park, on the other side of Cleveland, with its bright lights of frozen yogurt shops and trendy restaurants. We walked back to school and collected our books and bags from our lockers and took his dad's Caddy.

He pulled into the garage next to a Volvo and shut the engine down. We didn't talk as we walked up the stone path leading to the front door.

"We have to . . . keep it quiet, okay? My mom's been sick."

"No probs. What about your dad? Is he here?"

Brady used his key and I followed him into the entryway. I slipped off my shoes and set them on the shoe rack next to his, and I took in the delicacies of expensive-looking decor. The hallway runner alone looked like some serious shit.

Brady hung his key on a line of brass hooks. "Dad"—he was whispering now—"Dad left us the house, left us the car, and basically just left us."

"I'm sorry. When?"

"Last summer," he said.

"Sounds familiar. Except all my dad left us was a pile of bills and dirty laundry," I said.

Brady led me through the hall that opened up to a massive, shiny kitchen. I smoothed my hand over the marble countertop.

I sat on the stool and watched as Brady pulled out a pot, butter, milk, and mac 'n' cheese. "Gourmet. You watch those cable cooking shows?" I said.

"Oh, you wait." He opened the fridge and pulled out tomatoes, hot dogs, and extra cheese.

"Oh my. You're a fancy chef," I said.

"You have no idea."

We ate at the wooden table that could seat ten at a dinner party. Brady even set out a placemat with matching cloth napkins for us. Extra fancy.

I took my first bite. The hot 'n' cheesy started to burn my tongue and then my throat. I gulped down some milk, served in a wine glass, so I was still gulping when she stepped into the room.

"Oh, hello," she said with a sweetness that didn't match her hangover clothes and yellowed cigarette smile.

"What are you doing up?" Brady said.

She cackled. "It's morning."

"It's nearly five . . . p.m.," Brady said calmly.

"Well, I woke up. And so I'm up. Don't worry. I'll just grab some breakfast and be out of your hair. You can whore around when I'm done."

"Mom."

I stood up. "Maybe I'll go." No one seemed to hear me.

A cigarette and a lighter appeared out of nowhere. From her robe? That seemed like a check-off on some quiz for "Ten signs you smoke too much."

She lit up and took in a deep drag. "Such a pretty face," she exhaled. "You're a sucker for a pretty face Brady . . . just like your father."

Brady's cheeks were blotched with anger, but he didn't respond. I couldn't leave him. It would look like I was on her side. I sat down again.

Brady's mom disappeared with a bowl.

"She doesn't like me," I said.

"No, she doesn't like my dad. I look just like him.

Everything I do reminds her of him. But I would never be like him; there's a special place in hell for a cheater. She never used to be like this. What happened with your dad?"

"I don't know if he cheated. There were so many lies, we stopped asking the questions. Drugs, gambling . . . who knows? I even caught him stealing my dog-walking cash off my dresser." I surprised myself. I didn't even give that info away to Cooper.

"That's bad. You have brothers and sisters? Or was there just you to steal from?" he asked, interlacing his fingers with mine. I let him because it felt nice.

"My brothers were both out of the house by then. I'm sure Dad stole from them when they were home, but we didn't really talk about it. Even to each other. Then there's Henry. He was still pretty young when my dad split."

"That's rough for him."

"Yeah, except he doesn't miss him or get pissed because he never knew him."

"He will. You get along with your little brother?"

"Henry? He's my little angel." I smiled just thinking about him. "I was eleven when he was born. I used to pretend he was mine."

"Aw."

"Are you an only child?" I said.

"Could you tell? My mother has never been all that maternal. She got smart after me and made the doctors tie her tubes, even though she was only twenty."

"That's sad. Were you lonely?"

"No. There were always cleaning ladies around."

I must have made a face because he laughed.

"Just kidding." Brady sighed. "Let's get out of here. I'll drive you home."

×

We rode in silence. When we got to my driveway, Brady threw the car in park and jogged around to meet me as I closed my door. I opened my mouth to thank him and say good-bye, but he was already talking.

"You sure you didn't know about Cooper and Marilyn before he died?"

I blinked. He was asking me if I lied. Asking me if I cheated with a cheater. Wasn't exactly the good-bye I was expecting. "No. I guess part of me is still hoping it's all crap talk. I get the feeling Marilyn lies."

"Yeah. That's what I thought. Just checking."

He nodded for me to continue. "I don't even know which would make me hate her more. If she was messing around with him or if she's just trying to get everyone to believe it."

"Why would she do that?"

"I don't know. For attention?"

He tipped his head. "But really?"

"What? You think I'm in denial?"

"All I know is that no one's perfect. Even after death, despite what everyone tries to get you to believe." He stepped forward and slipped an arm around my waist. "Even if he's dead, it's okay to think bad about him."

I didn't like the conversation. I pushed against his chest, but he didn't let go. His eyes bore into me.

"You really think he was with her?" I asked.

"Yes. I know he was. Don't you? When you really think about it?"

My mouth was hanging open, but when I tried to speak, my jaw just uselessly wagged.

"I'm sorry," he said. "You deserve better."

I pushed again and he released me. "I have to go."

"I feel bad that you weren't ready to hear that. Let me walk you in, okay?"

I didn't want him in. I needed to think, and inviting him seemed to send the wrong message. But it wasn't his fault. He was being honest.

I saw the glow of the TV in the front room.

"Let's go around back," I said.

I rounded the house to Landon's backyard. My backyard. And there she was. Marilyn.

On my deck, in my swing chair next to Mattie, laughing with Franklin and Greta. Damn, I forgot that they were coming. Franklin was on the bench seat with the back of Greta's head resting on his thigh. Mattie's arm rested on the back of the chair, behind Marilyn. He was smiling.

The cozy scene of friends gave me a stomachache. Marilyn was an integral part of this whole mess—not to mention a girl who may or may not have been screwing around with Cooper. My instinct was definitely seeing the virtues of hair pulling and sucker punches. In fact, holding back took every ounce of self-control.

As I stepped closer, Brady was right behind me. I'd almost forgotten he was still with me. Marilyn's laugh scratched the inside of my skull. I was trying on my friendly smile, but I guess my impatience needed an outlet because my foot began tapping on its own accord. "Are you guys comfortable? Can I get you some snackage?" I asked them.

The laughing stopped. Marilyn's face was priceless and I was sure I saw her inch away from Mattie. Any satisfaction this gave me seeped away when I noticed the rest of them taking their time making eye contact. No one said hello, and Franklin looked downright pissed.

Greta lifted her head off Franklin's leg to look up at me. "No. We went for pho." Her voice was flat, and she didn't look like she was going to offer me a hug.

"You didn't tell me you were going for pho. I love pho."

Franklin's eyes were cold when he looked at me. "We all have our secrets, right?" he said with a smile.

Greta sat up and leaned back into Franklin's extended arm. "Marilyn told us about you and Cooper."

"Helpful, that Marilyn," I said, keeping my gaze on Greta.

Marilyn spoke up, but her voice was so low I barely heard it. "I thought they must already know, since they're your friends."

"Yes, they are my friends," I said, still not looking at her.

"Supposedly," Franklin said.

I shot him a glare. "Do you have a problem?"

Franklin jumped to his feet, causing Greta to spill onto the deck. "Do I have a problem? From day one you were telling us what snobs everyone was at your school." He pointed his finger in my face. "Never be friends with them, you said."

I slapped his hand away. "You were telling me what snobs they were. And I wasn't friends with any of them."

Franklin jerked his shoulders. "Guess fucking them isn't the same as—"

I hadn't even realized he was moving until Brady's fist landed in Franklin's mush. Franklin tipped back a step. He wiped a couple dots of blood off his lip as Brady shook out his hand. Mattie didn't even get to his feet. He barely bothered to lean forward.

Greta wrapped her arms around Franklin.

Franklin broke into a huge grin, keeping his eyes on Brady, but his arms wound around Greta almost instinctually. "That all you got, buttercup?"

"You can say whatever you want about me, but don't talk to Cassie like that," Brady said.

Normally this kind of thing would have me riled. I didn't need a boy standing up for me. But I was so pissed at everyone else, I let it go.

"Well, let's get started on you, then," Franklin said.

I clasped my hand on Brady's arm and yanked him back a step. "Stop it. Can we focus? I'm still trying to help Gav."

"Oh, really? This is about Gav then? Not about Cooper?" Franklin said.

"It's about both. I'm trying to figure out who killed Cooper, to clear Gav. Obviously."

"So are we," said Marilyn.

I turned to her. We? Mattie sat there like a rock, not even looking at me.

"Great, let's get down to it then. Did you buy drugs from Gav? Oh, I'm sorry, I mean were you forced into buying from him?"

"I heard about Gav from Gobbers. He helped me buy from Gav. I was going through a lot of stuff and—"

"That's not what you told Cooper."

"Yes, it is. Cooper was just upset about me being so young and all, he blew it out of proportion. I feel horrible they went to beat up Gav."

"How can you lie like that! You loved Cooper going after Gav."

"No," she said, raising her voice. Her eyes filled with tears. "I felt even worse that the rift it caused may have been why Gav—"

"Stop talking! You don't feel bad at all, about anything. In fact, I'd like to see your phone. Cop told me whoever sent the text to get Cooper into the woods that night used a prepay. Is yours a prepay?"

Marilyn's mouth was hanging open. Tears began falling and her hands were shaking. "I didn't . . ." Then she fell into a bunch of sniffles. I was so not buying it.

She reached into her backpack next to her on the swing, until Mattie stilled her hand with his.

Franklin spoke up. "Leave her alone. It doesn't even matter. Lots of people have prepays. I have a fucking prepay. Anyone can get one, and no one would be stupid enough to keep the phone after sending a text and then killing the guy."

Marilyn stood. Her hands grasped her bag, and her eyes were glued to the deck. "I'm sorry if Cooper seeing me hurt you. It hurts me that he was seeing you, too."

There was something about her just then that made me silently call bullshit. And after looking to see I was the only one with eyes on her, she smiled. There weren't words, there was just me launching at her. Before I could get a claw into her, Mattie and Franklin closed ranks on me. I gave them each a push, but gave up. I folded my shaking arms in front of me. Brady scooped an arm around my waist, his nails digging into my side.

Marilyn's eyes so were big I thought they'd pop out.

I'm sure this was the closest she'd been to a fight.

There was only white-hot noise in my ears. I almost missed Brady telling Marilyn that he'd give her a ride home. Finally, when she was gone I could breathe.

"Can you believe that crap she's trying to put over?" I said.

The guys looked more ready for a fight than a talk. Which was fine; I was, too.

"I don't even care, but you should have told us about you and Cooper," Greta said.

I felt like I was on the outside of a glass house looking in. The pain in my chest came so sudden I had to resist the urge to look down for the dagger that must have been plunged into it.

"Mattie thinks—" Greta started.

"Mattie can shut up about his girlfriend, because I don't want to hear it," I said.

Mattie tipped his head, but held his silence.

I kept on. "You want to take her side, then take it. You want to throw away over ten years of friendship, then throw it. But she lies."

So do you.

I stared at him. He dared me to speak. I shoved Mattie as hard as I could. "Is that what you think? Say something." Nothing.

It was never Mattie against me. We were always on the same page. Always on the same team. Always.

"Marilyn twisted Cooper into believing lies, and now she's twisted you into trusting her over me? I know that I lied. I know I've been doing this without you, but I had to! I'm doing all of this for us. To fix us." My voice cracked on the last word. But when I looked around, it occurred to me that maybe it was too late, maybe I wasn't part of "us" anymore.

As if confirmation was needed, when I looked one more time at Mattie, I realized he was purposefully blanking me. Blocking me out.

For the first time in my life, I couldn't hear Mattie.

Chapter 22

I struggled up the stairs to my room. I was exhausted and freezing. I debated between a hot shower or flopping face first into bed. But as I stood in the hall, an aching feeling overtook them both: loneliness. I crept into Henry's room and lay down next to him. I pulled the extra blanket from the foot of his bed over my shoulder. His eyes peered at me through the dark. "You sleep here tonight, Cassie?"

"Is that okay?"

"It's okay," he said, patting my arm. "Where is Mattie?"

"Mattie . . . had to go home."

"Mattie is your best friend, but you're my best friend," Henry said.

My throat tightened. "You're my best friend, too. See, you can have more than one favorite."

"Like loving chocolate and strawberry ice cream. You can love them both?" he said.

"Right," I said. "You love them both."

The nightmares kept coming all night. Cooper called out to me over and over in the woods before I finally gave up on sleep. Afraid I'd wake Henry, I went to my room and sat in my window well watching stars and cars until it was time to shower.

I dressed deliberately. I pulled out the uniform slacks from my bottom drawer. I snapped the price tag off from the waistband. Up until now I'd only worn the skirts, trying to fit into what I thought was the image I needed to get by. It didn't matter though. I was fully outed, so there wasn't any use in pretending anymore. I brushed my hair out and twisted it up in a band. If I was going to walk into a battlefield, I wanted my battle gear to be comfortable.

I kept rubbing the scratchy sand out of my eyes, but that wasn't helping me wake up. It only served to make my eyes sore and puffy. I sipped my coffee with cream that was really more cream with coffee and stared at the Captain Shakes cereal box. As the messages on the box began to morph into a dream, I was shaken back into reality two inches before my nose met the milk in my cereal bowl.

"I'm up," I said. I glanced at my mother who was now sitting next to me.

"Are you okay?" she said, placing a hand on my free wrist.

I looked at her. "Now? After all that's happened, now you ask?"

She leaned back in her chair. "We thought that you were doing fine, coping with all of your friends?"

I hated that she referred to herself as "we" even when Landon wasn't in the room. And the mention of my "friends" made the tears come. I dropped the spoon and slapped both hands to cover my eyes.

"Cassie? What is all of this? You're not sleeping, are you? At least not well. I've heard you thrashing around," she said.

I wrapped my hands around my mug and sniffed a few times, trying to ward off a breakdown.

"Did you and Gav have something . . . special?" she said.

I sighed. "He's my friend, Mom. We grew up on the same street, remember? And now he's in jail for murder."

"Yes, and we realize how hard that must be for you. Gav is still your friend. We are all capable, under the right circumstances—"

I slammed my hand down on the counter. "He didn't do it! Why does everyone find it so easy to believe that he could kill someone?"

"Cassie, the police—"

"Got it wrong!"

She pursed her lips before trying again. "But if—if—he did it, he is still the same person. Even if he made a mistake."

"Mistake? What is wrong with you people? You don't just go from being a nice, normal person to being capable of bashing someone's brains in."

"He's still your friend. You can still love him," she said.

"Mother, if he killed Cooper, he can go to hell without me saying another word to him."

I tried to get my breathing under control.

"Did you know him?"

She was trying. But it was too much to cover in a ten-minute heart-to-heart. I kissed her cheek. "I have to go."

×

It was raining again. I pulled my hoodie forward and had gone a few steps wrapped in my brain fog before realizing there was a car parked at the end of the driveway. I stopped walking and squinted, trying to see if it was Limey.

It was Brady's Caddy. The window buzzed down on the passenger side, and Brady leaned over the passenger seat.

"Want a ride? I got breakfast," he said.

I got in, snapped my seat belt, and reached for the sausagey-smelling sandwich.

I munched, scooting farther back into the leather seat.

"This is weird, but why is my butt hot?" I said.

He glanced at me as he hit the turn signal. "Heated seats," he said.

"Nice." I took another bite of sandwich. "I thought I was having a stroke."

He pulled into the lot at school. It was like being at a different place. I don't think I remembered seeing the school from this angle before, though I must have—those early days of registration or whatever. It was like a castle in the middle of the city.

It wasn't lost on me that we were going into this together. That whatever the day faced, Brady had my back. I got out of the car before there could be any awkward will-he-or-won't-he-try-to-kiss-me moment.

We walked shoulder to shoulder as we parted the sea of pointed stares.

I spotted Marilyn in the hall ducking into the bathroom. I had to keep after her. Not with a crowd, but just her and me. I went after her, until Brady snagged my elbow. "I'll wait for you."

I followed her in. I checked the other stalls to make sure we were alone, and then waited for her to flush.

"Stalk much?" she said as she came out of the stall. I noted the black eye she was trying to hide under heavy foundation. It was new; she didn't have it last night. She glanced at the door behind me, already looking for an escape.

"Where'd you get that black eye?"

At the sink, she glanced at me through the reflection in the mirror. "News flash? I don't even know you." She pulled off a handful of paper towels. Again, her eyes went to the door.

"I know. I don't know you, either, and I don't trust you," I said.

"Obviously. Geez. Anything else you'd like to accuse me of? I didn't send the text! I really liked Cooper." Her eyes moved away from mine as she said it. It was a personal admission, and maybe there was some insecurity there. But I'd read something once about liars lying like they tell the truth and telling the truth like they're lying.

I stepped in closer. "I know. You guys had a thing," I said, watching her closely.

She looked me in the eye. "Yeah. We had a thing. It was getting serious, too." Lie?

"Were you with him that night?" I asked.

Her eyes shifted to the left. "No." Truth?

I took another step toward her. "Who gives you those bruises?"

She didn't answer, but looked at me. There was something there in her eyes. Something . . . come on! I'd have to be a code breaker to crack the meaning of that look.

I waited. I thought, maybe foolishly, she was about

to give me something real.

The door bumped on its hinges behind me, like someone rested their weight against it. A shadow moved in the crack beneath the door—maybe Brady was getting impatient.

When I looked back at Marilyn, I knew the moment, if there had been one, had passed. I watched her root around in her bag until she found a pack of smokes. Her hands were shaking. With the cig in her mouth, she had to use both hands to steady the lighter to get the flame to meet the end.

"You know," she said, inhaling a shallow breath before blowing out the smoke. "Between you and me? Gav hated Cooper, even before the whole thing at the park."

"That doesn't mean he'd kill him."

"Doesn't it? Maybe he didn't mean to kill him? Or maybe you didn't know him as well as you thought." She kept her eyes down as she continued to smoke. Truth?

That got me. "You don't know my friends better than I do."

She rolled her eyes and added a sneer. "Mattie's a great kisser." She blew out a puff of smoke. "Did you know that?"

I tried to keep my face as still as possible, but it's hard not to wince when someone sucker punches you in the gut.

She shrugged innocently. "You better go. The bell's

about to . . ." And then it did. Ring.

I walked out. Defeated.

Brady was waiting for me outside. He stepped away from the wall he was leaning against. He reached out and squeezed my shoulder. "What did you find out?"

Cold panic was starting to melt the numb. "I got nothing."

"Huh. Well, we'll just . . ."

"What? Tell me what we'll just do. Because all I got is theory. No one is talking, and I'm losing . . . everyone."

"I'm not going anywhere," he said.

I wished it was enough. I wished it felt like something.

"What if we can't find something and they keep Gav? Or we can't find anything because . . . what if . . . what if he did it?" I hated that Marilyn of all people had planted a thought in my head, and that it was actually taking root.

Brady was silent. It felt like what people must refer to as rock bottom. Things couldn't get any worse.

✕

But they did. I failed my math test. Bombed. I hadn't done any of the homework all weekend and had forgotten about the test. I was still holding the test in my hand fourth period when I realized Sister Rita was standing next to my desk. "Everyone's handing in their papers, Cassandra. Where is yours?"

Fuuuuuuuck.

I had completely forgotten to write my paper on affirmative action (why it's not always good, but sometimes great). I hadn't written a single word. I opened my mouth to say something, but the whole world felt like a lead X-ray vest. Which is to say: heavy.

Instead of words, the tears came again. They'd snuck up on me. I smacked my hands in front of my face, as if that was going to hide it. There was nothing but silence surrounding my pitiful squeaks, until I heard the ripping of paper. I slid my hands down and sniffed. Sister Rita had placed a pass on my desk. I picked it up and got my messenger bag from the back of my chair.

On the way to the nurse, Hailey crashed into me coming out of the peer counseling office. "Sorry," she said, stepping back.

I wiped at my face, relieved, I guess, that she wasn't threatening me or rubbing it in. "Yeah. Sorry."

"Hey," she said.

I looked back.

She was fidgeting. "I got a free period. You . . . have time to talk? I've been trying to catch you alone."

She wanted to talk to me? I looked around to make sure Devon wasn't with her. "Sure."

Hailey led me down to the music hall, somewhere I don't spend a lot of time, being so musically challenged and all. She opened the door of the band room.

"We can duck in here. Miss Perkins is good about us using the room," she said.

Us? Hailey was a band nerd? Interesting.

The room was empty, save the abandoned cluster of chairs, stands, and sheets. And a couple of instrument cases on the floor next to the piano. Hailey went in first and I checked around behind me one more time. I didn't really fancy getting jumped in the music room.

Hailey plopped down next to the piano and hugged her knees, watching me as I sat facing her. I crossed my legs, and she did the same. She was pretty, even with the heavy eye makeup.

I wondered about her. I never saw her in the flock of girls that followed Cooper's trio around. I only saw her with the guys, or just with Devon.

"Jenna told me you were in the peer counseling office looking through the binder. Did you find what you were looking for?" she said.

My cheeks burned. She had an edge to her voice, but not much of one. I could've lied, but I didn't really see the point. Hailey was talking to me. "I heard about Cooper kissing you, so I wanted to know what was going on in those meetings."

"What does that have to do with Cooper being killed?"

"You having a thing with Cooper gives Devon a motive," I said.

"Your thing with Cooper and the fact that your

friend threatened to kill Cooper gives your friend a motive, too," she said.

I sighed. It wasn't the same, but she had a point. "I understand why Gav is a suspect. But he's my friend. I don't believe he did it. Or at least I'm trying really hard to not believe it. I have to give it a shot. Try to find something else that makes sense."

She didn't say anything for a while. Thinking. I'd bet a million dollars she was thinking about whether she should trust me.

I tried again. "This is me. Being honest. I can't figure out who did it without knowing for sure who didn't. Help me cross Devon off the list."

She sat up straighter and leaned forward. "Okay. I didn't have a thing with Cooper. I kissed him. That was it. I love Devon, but he is clueless what to do when I'm upset. He doesn't know how to be emotional, himself. You know? He's not really a feelings kind of guy."

"I'm not so sure that's true. He has anger nailed."

She almost smiled. "Well, anger is a bad substitute for sadness."

"Was he angry when he found out about you and Cooper?" I asked as gently as I could.

"He was angry at himself. He said he felt like he had failed me. He's the one who wanted me to go to peer counseling in the first place, because when my mom got sick he had nothing for me but clichés and awkward back patting. He thought it was so great they were moving me to Cooper. Cooper could deal with that part of me. And he did. Cooper is—was—very . . . sensitive."

I nodded, even though it hurt.

"Devon just felt defeated. He was always measuring himself against Coop, and coming up short in his mind. We never really worked through it, the whole kiss thing. We just put it behind us—sort of."

"A wound never healed can only . . . fester?"

This time she laughed. "Gross. But, true."

"And he doesn't have an alibi."

"Yes. Yes, he does," she said. "With me."

"Wait. You're conveniently giving him an alibi now? You can't do that."

"He's always had one; it's just not very . . . convenient or pretty. But if you keep stirring, we're going to have to give it up," she said.

"Why isn't it convenient?"

"Sometimes the alibi is only slightly less incriminating than the crime," she said.

"What are you talking about? If you're going to tell me, you're going to have to actually tell me."

"Devon came home with me. My mom is in the hospital. Devon was mad at me and Cooper still. We fought about it at the Flame. So what does he do? Gets shit-faced with my father. And then my father starts yelling at him about being a bad boyfriend and kicks him out. Devon drove home drunk."

"Ever hear the one about how a girl always ends up dating her father?"

"Yuck."

"So Devon lied?"

"Devon could be kicked off the team. He could be kicked out of student council. My father could get arrested or sued. And my mom would be pissed. Any way I can imagine it in my head it looks ugly, so I told Devon to lie if anyone asked. He shouldn't need an alibi anyway. Cooper was his best friend."

"You don't think he could have killed Cooper?" I asked.

"There's no way he could have done it. He loved Coop. We all loved him. Besides, Devon didn't leave my house until almost four a.m. But even if he didn't have an alibi, I'd believe in him. Like you believe in your friend."

I nodded. I believed her. Or I wanted to believe her. If it was all true, I was glad for Hailey that Devon didn't do it. But it also meant I was still no closer to figuring out who did kill Cooper. I had to keep at it. I had to believe it. For Gav.

×

After school, Brady found me in the field facing the woods. I stood right up against the police tape, the trees less than five feet away. I'd spent the afternoon in the nurse's office trying to think. Mom wasn't answering her phone, and Landon wouldn't give them permission to let me leave early even though I pleaded I had "girl issues." He'd said to "tough it out."

"I need it down."

I turned my head toward the voice. Headmaster Spanders was talking to the security guard and pointing to the barricade still blocking the path to the football field.

The wind blew again, and I could catch only a handful of his words. "—thousand people here Friday—won't have them traipsing down Snelling—need the barricade down."

Brady came over to stand next to me on grass littered with leaves. The breeze snaked down my collar.

I rested my hands on the police tape that trembled in the wind and closed my eyes.

The day after they found Cooper, the cops were checking out two locations: the path, and somewhere in the woods. What if the initial blow happened on the path? I could still see chalk and the holes where bits of concrete were extracted. I pointed. "Limey said there were bits of the phone found there. From when he fell, or where the phone was stomped on by the killer. But Cooper was found in the woods." I looked over to the left side of the path. "What took him into the woods?"

"He was moved? Dragged?" Brady guessed.

"There was blood on the path. He was bleeding. If he was already dead, moving him off the path wouldn't have stopped the night security from finding him for very long. I think he ran." I shivered. "I think he got hit the first time on the path. The killer got Cooper's phone and smashed it on the ground, or maybe it got smashed when Cooper fell. But then Cooper tripped him, or kicked him or something to give himself enough time to stumble into the woods. He was chased. Maybe he tried to make a call, but the phone was broken. Or maybe he dropped it or threw it so the killer couldn't get rid of it. But eventually he couldn't run anymore. The trail of blood led the killer right to him."

I sucked in a breath that I hadn't realized I needed.

"Maybe his phone is still in the woods," I said.

Brady put a hand on my arm. "The police have combed all through there, Cassie. If the phone was there, they would have found it. It makes more sense that it's gone. Could have been dumped in the river for all we know. And even if it wasn't, what good does a broken phone do?"

"The SIM card might not have been damaged and it would have the text. The phone could have the killer's fingerprints if he touched it. . . . Do you even watch *CSI*? They can get someone's whole life from a phone!"

"Even if you could find the phone, and the text existed in some way, have you considered that if it was Gav or Franklin or—"

I glared at him before he could say "Mattie."

He held up his hands. "I'm just saying, maybe it isn't the best idea to go looking for it. Maybe you don't really want to find out what's on the phone, or who it leads to."

Chapter 23

Brady had offered me a ride, or even to walk with me, but the thoughts I was having were too thick for company. I wandered around, window shopping on Grand Ave. I paused in front of some kind of sports-specialty store and wondered if it was somewhere Cooper had liked to go. I pulled out our pictures again. It was starting to be a thing that they kept finding their way into my pocket every day. But looking at him now brought a fresh stab of anger. I stuffed the pictures back in my pocket. I hated that everyone accepted he was with Marilyn. Maybe that's what I should be doing, too. But it just didn't feel right. The way he was with me didn't feel like a line. I didn't want it to be.

I was angry at him for dying. I made up with him. I said I was sorry, and he left anyway. Obviously it wasn't his fault, or his choice, but the anger was still there.

I sighed. These thoughts were no good. Things happened for a reason, isn't that what people were always saying? Maybe it was apparent from the start I wasn't meant to be with Cooper, that we'd never go the distance. But was he meant to be killed? Was that fair? That we never even had a chance to try?

The streetlights clicked on and I realized I had circled back to my neighborhood. I hated how soon it got dark this time of year.

When I reached the end of my driveway, a dog barked in the distance. I had that weird being-watched kind of feeling.

Lengthening my strides, I pulled my phone out with one hand and reached for the garage code buttons with the other.

"I need to talk to you."

I spun around, flattening myself against the garage door, my phone falling onto the driveway.

Gobbers was in front of me, but he wasn't wearing any sign of the goofy smile or friendly, yet odd, manner he'd had the other day. He didn't say anything, or even look at me. He was busy rubbing the scruff off his bottom lip and looking up and down the street.

I caught my breath. "Are you lost or was there something you need? I'm trying to get ahold of someone, so . . ."

I kept my eyes on him as I squatted down and picked up my phone in case I needed to call 911.

He didn't make any move to stop me. He wiped his forehead with his sleeve. He was sweating. It was cold as shit out here and he was sweating.

"Are you okay?" I said.

He chuckled in that freaky way that made my skin crawl. "Why are you questioning everyone about me?"

"You know why. Gav didn't kill Cooper, and I'm trying to figure out who did."

He crossed his arms in front of him and started chewing skin on the knuckles of his left hand. "Why is Marilyn hanging out with your friends?"

"I guess they're friendly. If you have something to say, then say it, otherwise I got stuff to do."

He leaned in. "She lies."

"About what?"

"Everything. That's what she does. I wouldn't believe her if I were you," he said.

"So are you worried about me getting lied to? Or what she's going to tell me?"

"Sometimes . . . secrets are a good thing. A safe thing. I think you know what I mean."

I crossed my arms. "You came all the way to my house to *not* tell me something?"

He paused. "I bought the drugs from your friend Gav. For Marilyn. Happy? She wanted them and I bought them for her and got her in with Gav in case she wanted more. Marilyn always gets what she wants. She wants me to buy her shit? I do it. She wants Cooper to come to her rescue against the dealer? Of course he does."

"Then she tells some truth, because that's what she told us. What's the secret? Were you guys dating?" I said.

He stopped moving. "Who?"

I smiled. Now we were getting somewhere. "So you buy the drugs, then what? She gets nervous? Angry? Why did she tell Cooper she was forced into it? Just playing the damsel?"

He shrugged. "Maybe he caught her with it? I don't know."

"Was there something going on between her and Cooper?" Someone had to know. I sure as hell wasn't going to take Marilyn's word.

"Heck if I know. She wants everyone to believe it. That's her thing. Tell a sob story—dead grandma, abusive ex—and get everyone feeling sorry for her. I don't even know if that shit is true. Only half of what she says is true. But she'll do whatever she needs to, use whatever she has to, then when she's gotten what she wants, she cuts them loose."

"She got what she needed? A secret?"

He nodded. "She collects them."

"Why?"

"She's twisted." He shook his head. "My dad would

kill me if he knew." He was no longer looking at me. His mind was somewhere far away.

"Buying drugs? Or murder?" I asked.

He moved toward me so swiftly I thought I'd have to get into knee-to-the-crotch defense mode. But instead of reaching for me, his hand went like claws into his own head.

"You can't go around saying crap like that!" He threw his hands down and took a step back, leaning against the garage door. "I know what you think, but this has nothing to do with me! Leave it alone."

I had to pin him down. "It's hard to leave it alone. You had to have been pissed! She uses you, blackmails you, and then, like you said, cuts you loose to go for Cooper? Come on. Give me something. Tell me something real." My heart was throbbing in my throat.

His lips drew into a tight line. "You have to leave it alone."

It was a warning, and my whole body started this shiver thing. I took a step back just as a flash of headlights streamed over us.

My stepdad's Saab was pulling in. He beeped twice and I could barely see his hand at the front of the dash doing a wave. The garage door started to creak open behind me. Gobbers stepped through the light beams and into the dark of the neighbor's lawn on the other side and was gone.

Brady drove me to school again the next day. I made deals with my teachers about work I'd missed, not really knowing if I'd be able to come through on the new deadlines. After the last bell I met Brady at the loading dock. He was staring at me through my silence.

"What's up? You've barely said two words all day," he said.

"Sorry. Distraction. Gobbers showed up in my driveway last night."

His eyes got wide. "Why?"

"He was freaking. He might be taking a page out of Devon's—"

"Did he hurt you? What did he want?" His voice was rising.

I shook my head, feeling ridiculous. Just because it felt like a threat didn't mean it was . . . threatening. Did it? I didn't want Brady going to fisticuffs with his BFF over me if I was assuming too much. "I'm fine, he didn't even touch me. He was just amped up. Something about him and Marilyn. He said he was worried about her lying to me."

"About what? The drugs?"

"I don't think so because he admitted he bought them for her," I said. "It sounds like she threatened him with something. Or maybe he doesn't want it to get out that they had a thing?"

"Gobbers and Marilyn had a thing?" he said.

I lowered my voice. "I don't know."

He shook his head. "Doubt it. He's not exactly her type. She goes for ringleaders, not second-string tackles."

"Do you think it's possible Marilyn texted Cooper that night?" I asked him.

He threw up his hands. "I don't know. Someone did."

"Why is it so hard to believe? She's done it before—getting Cooper to come to her 'rescue.'" He didn't say anything so I kept going. "I bet you a hundred million dollars Gobbers was there with Marilyn. She calls Cooper on the sly, he shows up . . . a fight breaks out—"

He was shaking his head. "You really hate her, don't you?"

"Yes! But it's not about that. This makes sense, Brady."

"This isn't a game of Clue. You can't go around accusing people of murder without proof," Brady said.

"I'd have it if I had Cooper's phone," I said.

The shivers were gliding up my neck, tickling my hairline again. I closed my eyes and tried to hold on to the thought and pull it closer. The killer must have destroyed the phone. That would be the obvious choice. But what if he hadn't? Couldn't? Not like couldn't physically, but what if he didn't have a chance? I thought about the two locations. On the path and in the woods. Where it started was not where it ended.

Brady's voice interrupted my thoughts. "Let's run

the list again. Besides Gobbers and Marilyn, who do we have?"

"Eli and Devon?"

"Eli still doesn't have an alibi," he said.

"True. But . . ."

"You don't sound fired up about this possibility," he said.

I shrugged. "It doesn't feel right."

"Okay. What about Devon? Clear motive, no alibi, and ready to kill at any moment."

I thought about what Hailey said, but decided to keep the alibi she had for him to myself for the moment. Besides, all I had was her word. "It makes sense on paper, with him being all hacked off about Cooper and Hailey, and semipsychotic, but . . . I don't know. It doesn't feel right, either."

Brady sighed. He adjusted his glasses. I waited.

"You know why it doesn't feel right?" he asked, except it sounded like a statement.

"Why?" It felt anything but obvious to me.

"Because they're all Cooper's friends. Gobbers and Marilyn, too. It doesn't feel right because none of the people on the list hated him."

He was right.

Brady stepped forward and placed his hands on my shoulders. "I think it's time you think about who does hate him."

My eyes snapped shut. I couldn't do it. "I can't.

Brady . . ." My voice cracked.

"I know, but—Cassie, look at me."

I opened my eyes. Brady was intent behind his glasses. "You need to be honest with yourself. Who can you trust? Does Gav have an alibi? Franklin? Mattie? I've trusted you completely as we've gone through my friends, now I think we have to go through yours. Honestly."

"I don't know if I can. If I don't trust them—"

I had to clamp down on the words and my eyes again as they were pooling with tears.

"You need to trust *me*." I felt Brady's hands on my neck, weaving up the back of my hair. I opened my eyes to see him close, so close, and closing in.

"We're going to figure it out," he said, his breath warm on my lips. "Together."

His hands were strong against the back of my head, so I couldn't twist away as he pressed his lips on mine.

Brady's grip loosened with the sound of footsteps behind us. I pushed him away.

Behind me, Mattie stood there watching us.

"What are you doing here?" I said, stepping away from Brady. I could feel the burn starting on my cheeks. Hot panic was spreading like a rash through the inside of my chest.

He came close enough to reach out and pull at my arm. *We need to talk.*

"He shouldn't be here," Brady said sharply.

Mattie glared at Brady over my shoulder and stepped in close to me.

"Not now," I said to Mattie, avoiding his eyes. My voice came out in a whisper. I didn't know which was worse—that I was kissing Brady in front of Mattie, or that I was contemplating putting Mattie and my best friends on the list.

Mattie pulled me in closer, steering me away from Brady. He bent down so his temple grazed mine.

When? When is the right time?

He didn't just mean the talking. There was always something or someone between us; Cooper and Brady were just lately. "Don't do this now," I said.

When? he asked again. He shifted his forehead, waiting until he had my eyes connected to his. Everything around us became fuzzy, and all that was clear was his face in front of me. But panic was already setting in.

Never, was what I wanted to say. People leave. Dads leave. Boys die. It would never be the right time to risk what Mattie and I had—or risk losing my heart completely. Mattie was not a loss I could survive. I crossed my arms and stepped back, pulling my arm away from his grip.

"Devon will kick his ass. Not that it would take much," Brady said, from what felt like a million miles away.

I kept my eyes on Mattie. I took the pain and I rolled it into a fireball of anger. It was easy. Who did Mattie think he was trying to throw me off balance?

I wasn't going to let him make me feel bad for kissing Brady, either.

"I thought I told you guys to stay off campus."

He didn't say anything. I wasn't even getting a rise out of him. I kept on. "The front of the school with witnesses was one thing, but catching you out here alone? Are you stupid? Devon wouldn't hesitate to kick some ass if he didn't think he'd get caught." I clenched my jaw and tried to look pissed.

Mattie just looked at me until it hurt. He stepped in with a wicked smile, his hand over his heart. He was pissed. *Protecting me?* His eyes slid to Brady. *Or just can't wait to get back to making out with him?*—

I heard the smack and felt the sting on my hand before my brain caught up to what I'd done. Mattie touched the redness on his left cheek with his fingertips.

"Go!" I yelled.

He went.

I turned around to face Brady. It took a moment before the adrenaline cooled and the reality sunk in with a gasp.

Brady was next to me. He was saying, "It's okay, it's okay," and touching me, but all I could think about was what a complete bitch I was. I'd never hit Mattie.

I stood there until the sound of screeching tires scratched through the air, then another set, and then the impact of crashing metal.

My throat constricted. I wasn't one for praying, but I prayed, I bargained, and I pleaded. To God, angels, Buddha, the Universe—anyone who would listen:

Not. Mattie.

Then, I ran.

Chapter 24

I was moving. I sprinted to the front of the school and toward the gate. People were swarming toward Snelling Ave. Some were yelling.

We couldn't get through the crowd that funneled onto the crosswalk. Headmaster Spanders and a couple of teachers finally broke through as the sirens started to blare. An ambulance pulled up and one of the medics was shouting for people to back off. The teachers moved in to direct people away from the street. The crowd started to peel away, but the buzz was deafening. I lost track of Brady. Someone in front of me turned to speak to someone beside me. "Gobbers. He got hit by a Smart car."

I exhaled and all my muscles loosened. I felt guilty for my relief. Two cop cars pulled up with an ambulance. Another sounded in the distance.

"He's alive," someone called back, and everyone around me started buzzing again.

I heard a familiar voice. "That curb gets a little slippery." I found Devon standing next to Eli. He saw me looking. "Watch your step," he said.

I swallowed. Before I could respond, I heard my name being called behind me.

"Cass?" I swung around to see Greta. "Thank goodness." She hugged me, and if my arms hadn't felt like a million pounds I would have considered hugging her back. I tried to find Devon and Eli again, but they had moved through the crowd.

"Where's Mattie?" I asked.

"Uh . . ." She jerked her thumb over her shoulder. "He's back at the van with Franklin." She looked at me. "Come on, we'll give you a ride."

Did she know about the slap? I didn't ask, I just let her pull me along by my hand.

Mattie was leaning against the side of the van; the driver's seat was empty. I could still see the redness on the left side of his face. It made my eyes sting to know that I caused it.

It could have been Mattie.

Greta released my hand as we reached the van. I

kept my head down as I leaned my head into Mattie's chest. After a painful eternity, I felt him pat my back.

The side door whirred open, and Mattie let go. Greta, in the front seat, was either getting impatient or could see Franklin coming. I climbed in after Mattie and sat in the seat behind Greta.

Franklin pulled the door open on the driver's side. He had a baseball cap pulled low to his eyes. I guess that was his idea of a disguise, but it was wasted by his RESPECT THE PIPE T-shirt.

He didn't start the car right away. "That was awful," he said, his voice was low and gravelly.

He turned around in his seat. If Franklin was surprised to see me, he didn't show it.

He reached his fist toward me. I looked at it dumbly, before bumping it with mine.

"All right there, Cass?" Franklin said after clearing his throat.

"Yeah."

"You're looking ill. Not going to vom in my mom's van, are you?" Funny since he was looking about as pale as I'd ever seen him.

I gauged the level of acid in my stomach. "No."

He started up the engine and I tipped back my head against the seat. What the heck did Devon mean? Did he have something to do with the accident or was that what passed as humor in his world? Poor Gobbers. He might have killed Cooper, but it didn't mean he should be serving brain soup on Snelling Avenue. Did it? I thought how I'd prayed for it to be anyone other than Mattie.

There was whispering in the front seat and Greta turned around. "Are you really okay?" She turned back before I could answer. "Maybe we should call her mom?" Greta asked Franklin.

"I'm fine," I called out.

"Did you tell her what Marilyn said?" Greta asked.

I lifted my head to see who she was talking to—she was looking at Mattie.

Mattie shook his head.

Greta turned to me. "Marilyn used to go out with Brady."

I stilled. "Excuse me if I don't just take her word for it. Unless you have proof, I'll have to assume it's another one of her lies—"

"You can choose to, but we think it was a hard-won truth," Greta said. "Mattie's been working on her. It wasn't something she wanted to give up. I don't think it was the kind of relationship she was proud of."

She wasn't proud of it? Going out with Marilyn wouldn't be something I'd expect anyone to be bragging about.

"Be careful, Mattie," I said.

He looked at me sideways.

Greta spoke up. "I know you're hating on Marilyn,

and that's cool, but I think you need to deal with the fact that Brady lied. Big-deal lied."

"I know, I know," I said. And I could consider it. But I had lied, too.

Franklin pulled into my driveway. I hopped out and waited for Mattie, who climbed out behind me.

"Cass," Franklin called, climbing out from the van. "Look . . . ," he said when he was in front of me. "I'm sorry. Okay? I know you cared about that guy. About Cooper," he amended when he saw the look on my face. "I just . . . I still . . . it makes me angry. People like that always hurting us."

"Cooper isn't—wasn't—'people.' He was just Cooper. He wasn't perfect or an asshole. It's not black and white."

His arms gripped tightly across on his chest. "They were going to hurt Gav."

"Cooper was protecting someone. He was acting like an asshole to protect his friend. You of all people should get that."

He laughed. "I'm not always an asshole. I'm . . . trying."

"No, but you've been an asshole about this."

"You've changed."

I rolled my eyes.

"Maybe I am an asshole. But I will always wish the best for us and the shit for them."

I couldn't help it. I punched him in the chest.

"Ow!"

"Franklin, you need to shut up with all the 'us' and 'them' bullshit, or I'm gonna put you on the fucking suspect list."

He snorted. "Come on. I was joking!" He backed away and climbed into the driver's seat.

Fucking Franklin. There might be assholes at St. B's, but it wasn't lost on me that there were assholes who didn't go to St. B's.

Franklin leaned out his window. "Come on, Cass. Don't be a bitch."

"I'm a bitch, Franklin?" I walked over and grabbed a handful of rocks from under the bushes in the front yard. I started pelting them as hard as I could at the front of the van. I got about two or three off before Mattie wrapped his gorilla arms around me from behind, pinning my arms. By then Franklin had grasped the hint and backed out of the driveway. His tires chirped as he shifted it into drive, his foot already jamming the gas pedal.

Mom had left me a note about taking Henry to a theater class and out for Happy Meals afterward, so Mattie stayed. I did four hours of homework in my room, then ate three ham sandwiches to Mattie's two sandwiches while we watched a *16 and Pregnant* marathon on MTV. I don't remember falling asleep.

That night, in my dream, I was in the woods again.

Cooper was there sitting on our log. There was no blood this time and no hissing of my name. He was looking down at the ground. I called his name, but he still wouldn't look up. Without taking a step I was next to him.

He reached down to the hollowed-out knot and pulled out his phone. My bracelet was wrapped around it. "It's here, Cass," he said. But his voice was in my head, his lips didn't move.

"Who—?"

He shook his head before I could get out the rest of the question. "I never wanted to hurt you." His face wilted. "I'm so sorry. I never said it. About Gav. About the fight."

"No, no, no." I didn't want to waste precious seconds of whatever this was on sorry. I wrapped my arms around him, but it was like hugging sand. One moment he was solid, and the next he was slipping away.

I looked down and I was holding the phone with the bracelet. Tucked inside the leather strap was a torn piece of paper that said, "You can only trust one."

I was learning a lot about trust this week. But there was only one person I knew I could trust with my life.

The person who had given me that bracelet.

Mattie.

When I woke up in the morning, we were facing each other in my bed, his arm slung around me. Mattie. My best friend. He snored softly and I watched him breathe. I remembered the razor-like pain I felt when I thought it was Mattie in the street. I didn't want to find out if Gobbers did it. Killed Cooper. Or Devon. Or Eli. I didn't want to find out if anyone did it. Because it would end up being someone's best friend.

I peeled away from Mattie and headed downstairs.

When I got to the kitchen, I heard the sound of glass breaking in the living room. I froze. I leaned against the doorjamb and peered out. I didn't hear anything else except the usual bird chirping and car engines, but those sounds were louder than they should've been.

The curtain on the front window billowed in with the breeze. I tiptoed in, not really sure why I felt the need to be quiet. I made sure the dead bolt on the front door was locked.

Next to the TV, on the carpet, was a smooth rock as big as my fist with the word SLUT written on it in magic marker. Ice burst through my chest. I thought about Mattie still asleep in my bed, and the mess with Cooper, and being seen all around with Brady. Anyone could have gotten the wrong impression. Or maybe it was me who was doing this all wrong. I should have been drowning my sorrows in ice cream and girlie sleepovers. But Mattie was what I had.

Cold fear ran through me as I questioned everything and everyone again. I shook it away. I couldn't start questioning everyone I cared for or I'd go crazy. But maybe it would be a good day for a sick day. Maybe a nap and then go riding with Mattie. I needed a big-time mental health day.

Landon and Mom were already gone. I cleaned up the glass from the rug as best I could, then texted Mom that some kid I didn't recognize accidentally lost trajectory on his baseball. I also said I had cramps so she'd call me in sick—at least for the morning. I brought up some granola bars for Mattie and told him to text his mom to call him in, too.

I showed Mattie the rock. He got a Sharpie out of his bag and made the *Slut* into *Slob* and set it on my shelf. Only Mattie could make something bad into something funny in thirty seconds flat. But he couldn't make it all go away with a swipe of a marker.

He scratched at the shoulder of my shirt.

I sighed. "I don't want to do this anymore. I just want it all to be over. I want the cops to do their jobs and find a reason that Gav was a block off "

Mattie paused while the lightbulb lit above my head.

What?

"Gav was a block off Snelling. He wasn't coming from my school. And it wasn't the drugs Gobbers was so freaked about people finding out."

What do you mean?

I didn't answer right away, the thought still forming. "Greta was right. Gav was hiding something. He was hiding a boyfriend. And his boyfriend is hiding him."

I grabbed my shoes. The mental health day would have to wait.

Chapter 25

Mattie and I skated to Gobbers's house.

Something caught my eye on the curb in front of the house. I knelt down and pointed to the green paint that was scratched into the curb. Gav's green. Mattie nodded with big eyes. It had to be. We walked up the driveway and around to the back. Three cement stairs stood below the back door. With the absence of a railing it was perfect for tricks and grinding. I stooped and ran my fingers along the green streaks. I hadn't noticed them before, walking down the steps with Brady.

"What are you doing? Get away from there!" Gobbers's mom yelled at us through the back screen door.

I stood up from my crouch. "We need to talk to Jesse," I said, remembering her calling him that. "Is he here?"

"He doesn't need to talk to you," she said.

Gobbers appeared behind his mom. "It's cool, Mom." He opened the screen door and held it wide to let us step through. He had on a vest that Velcroed his right arm to his chest. There was a thick bandage on the side of his forehead.

"Twelve stitches," he said.

I peered past him, toward the front room, but there was no sign of his dad.

Gobbers stood back so we could come in. He led us downstairs.

"This is my friend, Mattie," I told him.

Gobbers nodded at Mattie.

We didn't sit. "The timing of all this is crap, but we had to talk to you," I said.

Gobbers stayed still, not responding.

"I know you lied about how you know Gav," I said.

He looked at me. Leaning against the back of his couch, the tension in Gobbers's shoulders seemed to double.

"The green paint outside is from his board. That green isn't factory. He's been here. So either it was part of a motive for killing Cooper—hiding your relationship—or you've just been killing Gav's alibi. Either way, it's totally pissing me off," I said.

I saw his Adam's apple bob before his eyes fell again. "I didn't kill Cooper."

"I know that. You need to tell the police you were here that night, and that Gav was here with you," I said.

I waited, but he wasn't saying anything else. "He's eighteen. They're going to have to charge Gav as an adult. Don't you even care?"

He closed his eyes.

I pushed again. "Do you care about Gav so little that you're going to let him take the fall for murder?"

"You don't think diving into traffic on Snelling Ave. shows I care?" he said dryly.

Diving? He wasn't pushed, he didn't trip. He *dove*. He did feel guilty. But guilt wasn't enough. "I didn't know . . . but it doesn't make me think you're brave." I swallowed. "It just confirms to me that you're a coward."

He opened his eyes, which were lined with tears.

"I'm sorry, but it's true," I said.

"You're right. But it's not that easy. I have to think about it. It's not just me. Gav hasn't told anyone . . . about us, right?" he asked.

"He's protecting you. But you shouldn't let him."

Gobbers passed his shaky hand over the bristles of his shaved hair. "It's my dad. He'd never—I can't—"

A knot tightened in my stomach.

"Not to mention my friends . . ."

"I understand. But even in the St. B's football world there has to be people who understand that you without a cheerleader on your arm is still you, right? Just think about it, okay?" I asked.

I felt bad enough for bullying Gobbers, but it needed to be done. Gav would need an alibi if I couldn't find the killer in time.

Gobbers followed us up the stairs. As I stepped out the back door, Gobbers stopped me with this voice. "You wanted to know about Marilyn and Cooper, right? Ask Eli."

"I'm not exactly friends with Eli," I said.

"He'll talk to you," Gobbers said. "I'll tell him to, okay? You want his number?"

I handed him my phone and he put Eli's number into my contacts.

"Thanks. For real. Your true friends aren't going to care about you and Gav. Brady never believed you killed Cooper."

His hand stilled where he was rubbing the back of his neck. He looked confused. "Why would I care what Brady thought?"

"You guys are good friends, right?" I asked.

"Good friends? No, I wouldn't say that. I've known him for a while. Is that what he said?"

I tried to think back. What had he said? The memorial party seemed so long ago. "No, no." I waved him off. "I must have just assumed it. Guess I got it wrong." Except that I wasn't sure.

Mattie and I rolled down the driveway, but as soon as we met the street he had my elbow.

That's it?

"What do you want me to do, call the cops?"

Yes!

"Gobbers is going to have to wrestle with his own conscience, and for now we have to let him. I do think he cares about Gav, and I also think Gav must care about him, or he would have been using the alibi from day one. The paint only proves he was here, not when he was here."

So what now?

"We have to figure out the rest. And I need Eli to help us. What time is it?"

Mattie looked at his watch, then turned his arm so I could see for myself.

"Let's go get something to eat," I said.

×

We slid into a booth at the Flame. I texted Eli, then set my phone on the table. I hoped he, like most people, checked his phone at lunchtime. I ordered a couple of Cokes and watched Mattie as he looked over the plastic coated menu.

My phone buzzed. Brady. **Evrything ok?**

I hit IGNORE and gave my phone a knock toward the salt shakers.

I glanced at Mattie. Better to get the business with him out of the way. I tucked my hands under my legs. "Marilyn has an alibi, but I still wonder about her role. If—if she had a role in this," I said, trying not to have any kind of a tone.

Mattie's eyes flashed over the top of the menu. He folded it up and set it in front of him. He lay his hands flat on top of it.

"And I have to figure out what's going on with Brady. I don't think he's been telling me the truth about everything."

He nodded in agreement. The waitress dropped down our Cokes. She reached into her apron and pulled out a stack of napkins and threw them down in front of me without a word.

Over Mattie's shoulder, I saw the door open from the street. Eli stepped in, his eyes locking on mine right away. Mattie glanced back and started to rub his hands on his jeans. He didn't like it, and it wasn't like I was digging on this awkwardness, either.

Eli, after hesitating when he reached our booth, sat next to me.

I scooted over to give him a buffer. I decided to skip over any uncomfortable greetings and introductions. "Forty minutes for lunch?" I said.

"Yeah," Eli said. "What about you?"

"Home sick. Going back after lunch," I said, though it was obvious.

Eli nodded as he glanced around. "Why did you text me?"

"I want to finish this. For Cooper. I want to figure out what happened, and I need your help. Why'd you come here?" I asked him.

"You invited me."

"Yeah. But why did you come? You hate me."

He sighed and twisted in his seat. "I don't hate you. I'm just not sure about you."

The waitress with her brows pencil-drawn too low, making her look angry, came over to give us a chance to order. Her smile with the angry eyebrows made it look like she was in pain.

"I'll just take some fries," I said, handing her back the plastic menu.

"Burger. Well," Eli said, doing the same.

Mattie shrugged, then pointed to his glass.

"Refill coming, sweetie," she said, picking up Mattie's menu from the table.

Mattie nodded as he stabbed his straw into the ice in his glass.

"Here's the deal," Eli said. "Like I told you before, I knew Cooper was seeing someone. I didn't know for sure until later on that the person was you. But I do know Cooper was wrecked over you. I mean wrecked. But I wasn't sure if it was mutual. Not until Devon accused you of scamming Coop. I don't think you're that good an actress. I could see it was real."

My heart was beating so hard it hurt. I spared a glance at Mattie who was looking decidedly not at me. "I don't know what we had, but it was real. I was real with him, and he was real with me. We just had a lot of shit against us. You didn't have to be such a dick about it."

"Can you blame me? Coop said you broke up with him," Eli said.

"That's because—"

"Yeah, yeah. Gav. That was dumb. Marilyn had us in a twist over that. Turns out it was a bunch of shit, like most of what she says." He rolled his eyes. "Gobbers said you wanted to know about them, about Marilyn and Coop?"

"I don't need to know." And it was suddenly true. What Cooper and I had was real. It was messy and it was mistimed, and ultimately tragic, but it was real. And that's all I needed to know. What was between him and anyone else was beside the point, like whatever was between me and—

Mattie knocked on the table. I glanced at him, then at Eli's questioning glance. "Mattie wants to know if they were together."

He shook his head. "No."

"Just like that? No? Why are you letting her say it, then?" I asked.

"What am I gonna say? I was the only one who knew about you and Coop, and I wasn't sure you were worth sticking my neck out for. But now . . . I want to make sure whoever killed Coop is the one that rots in jail. If you don't think it was Gav, then I'll help you figure out who did it."

I glanced at Mattie. I trusted him, but I didn't trust her. "Marilyn—"

"Was with me," Eli said.

A piece of silverware clattered beneath our booth and I wasn't sure if it was me or Mattie who dropped it. We were both staring at Eli trying to figure out what happened.

He wasn't saying anything else.

"Sorry. I think we're just . . . we didn't know you guys had a thing," I said to break the silence.

Eli rubbed his hands together. "We don't. We didn't. It was just—" He scooted around in his seat, clearly uncomfortable with this narrative. "Cooper blew her off that day—the Friday he . . . died. Clear and harsh, no wiggle room for misunderstanding. He didn't want anything to do with her. She texted me, I don't know why—no, I do—to hurt Cooper probably. To make him jealous. She texted me when we were all still at the Flame. While we went back and forth, Cooper's phone buzzed on the table. I didn't even—"

Eli's voice broke and I kept my own eyes down to

give him a moment, but I selfishly hoped it didn't keep him from pressing on with his story.

"I didn't even look at him. I don't know if he was upset . . . or excited? I'm not even sure what he said to us. Devon was still bickering with Hailey. I just figured it was the girl he was seeing, meaning you, and that he was going to see you. So I thought what the hell, and I told Marilyn I'd come get her. We parked downtown by the river. Stayed there all night, and then woke up to my phone ringing: Hailey."

"You lied because you didn't want people to know?" I asked him.

"It was one night. Doesn't have to be everyone's business." He glanced at Mattie then over to me. "Marilyn's fun. Nice girl, too. But lies constantly. I don't think she can even help it. Though sometimes liars are the best at keeping secrets."

I couldn't deny that.

My own phone buzzed on the table. Brady.

Where are you

I cleared out the message without answering.

My knee bobbed.

"Was Brady here at the Flame that night—the night Cooper was killed?"

"Brady? No. Why?" Eli said.

Tingly shivers worked up the back of my neck. "Are you sure? One hundred percent?" There was no mistaking this. Brady may not like to talk about exes, and I may have misunderstood him being friends with Gobbers, but if he didn't have an alibi . . .

"I would have noticed. He doesn't hang with the crowd that comes here. He doesn't really hang with anyone that I know of. If there was someone new here I would have noticed," Eli said.

Mattie looked at me intently. He didn't know about all the lies, but he knew enough to know something was up. I shook my head at him. Later.

"What's up?" Eli asked, as if reading Mattie's mind after taking in our silent exchange.

"It's nothing. Just one of the many things I have to clear up," I said.

Even if Eli and Brady weren't friends, I couldn't risk something getting back to Brady. I downplayed with a grin and a shrug. I told Eli about the rock.

"You're becoming a target. Gav's not here, so people blame you. Like, guilt by association. I didn't know about it, if that means anything. But it could be someone is out to get you. You're not planning on going to the Homecoming Bonfire tonight, right? Might be a good night to stay home."

The Bonfire. The perfect distraction. The tape would be down and the path would be clear, just like Spanders had said. Tonight. I could get the phone tonight. And my bracelet.

My knee started to bob again, and I stilled it with my hand. "Thanks for the concern. But I'm not staying home."

"Why not?" Eli asked.

"Because if the bastard comes after me, at least I'd know for sure who it was."

They both froze and looked at me. Mattie still held the straw above the glass midstab. The waitress returned. She had smudged half of her left eyebrow right off. She set a burger in front of Eli, then the fries in front of me. I took two and slid the plate toward Mattie. He didn't touch them.

My phone buzzed again. Brady.

Chapter 26

I signed in at the office and let them know I was feeling better, then scooted off to afternoon class. There were two objectives for the afternoon: stay away from Brady, and plan out how to get to Cooper's phone—the only hope I had to prove who lured Cooper to the woods that night. I needed to get past the ropes and past the security guards or police or whatever they were, and get to that phone.

Last period. Gym. Brady caught me just outside the girls' locker room.

"Where have you been?" he asked.

The tone of his voice caused my shoulders to shake involuntarily. Or maybe not so much the tone as just his voice.

"Laying low," I said.

"Why? What happened?" he asked.

I looked at him. "Why do you think something happened?"

He smirked, like it was so obvious, it was funny. "Because you were gone all morning, and didn't answer any of my text messages. I was about to send a search party."

"Not true. I answered the third one," I said.

"Come on. Tell me. We're on the same team, right?"

I glanced around at the girls filing in and out of the locker room. This had to be fast or I'd be caught after the bell. I told him about the rock. I tried to gauge his face for any flicker of guilt, which didn't work because I'd barely had it out when he pulled me into a hug that smashed my face into his shirt pocket.

When he finally released me and glanced at his watch, my teeth were chattering. "I have to go." And I turned to do just that.

"What's wrong with your wrist?" Brady said from behind me.

"What?" I looked down and realized I was holding it with the opposite hand.

"What's wrong with your wrist?" he asked again. He reached out and took hold of my hand, drawing it toward him to have a look at my wrist. "You were rubbing it. You do that sometimes."

"Was I?" I tugged my arm, but he didn't seem to notice.

"Is it an itch? I don't see a rash."

I shook my head. "Lost my bracelet," I said.

"Must have been pretty special, for you to be physically missing it," he said dryly.

"It was."

"From Cooper?" he asked, as his grasp on my wrist tightened.

I twisted my arm in his hand. "No. From Mattie."

"Mattie? Ah. He has his way with girls, doesn't he?"

I felt like pressing him, being this close to the truth. Maybe he'd give something away. I stopped tugging and stepped toward him. "You mean Marilyn? Does that bother you?"

His eyes met mine, his eyebrows raised in surprise. He released my hand. "No," he said with a shake of his head. He lowered his eyes. "That's history."

So he admits it. "Did it end badly?"

"It just ended. Does it bother you?" He thought I was jealous.

"Just wondered why you lied," I said.

"You lied about Cooper."

"It was a secret relationship, hence the secret," I said.

"So was ours. You going to the bonfire tonight?" he asked.

I started to pull away. "I'm not sure," I said.

"I could pick you up?"

"I don't think . . ."

He was watching me. Waiting. For the lie?

"I don't want to. I want to wake up and have this whole thing be over. I gotta go," I said, pulling open the locker room door before he could say anything else.

He called after me. "I'll find you after school. I don't want you to be alone."

And he did. Find me. At my locker after school.

"What's that for?" I asked as I slammed my locker door.

"I bought you a Windbreaker at the school store," he said.

I stared at it. "I don't wear Windbreakers." I headed up the stairs to the front door, not wanting our time to linger any more than it had to.

"Not even when it's windy? Come on, I noticed you shivering earlier and it looks like rain. Just try it," he said, pressing it against my stomach.

I grabbed the jacket off him, if only to shut him up and stop from him touching me. I descended the front steps to the street and Mattie rolled up at the gate. Brady got very still. "What's this?"

"No big deal, but can we agree on some kind of split custody deal here?" I said.

"I don't think that's a good idea. I'll give you a ride home," Brady said, keeping my pace to meet Mattie.

Mattie shook his head. He tipped his head toward the school, then reached for my hand.

I wasn't sure about the hand holding, but he threw in a smile to lessen the blow. "He's got a point," I said to Brady.

"He had a point? He didn't say anything," Brady said, looking down at our clasped hands.

"He said we were in school together all day, so I should be with him tonight."

"I get days and he gets nights? Seems like I'm getting the short end of the stick," he said bitterly.

I looked at him. Did Brady know about Mattie staying over? He wasn't smiling and neither was Mattie. The wind was warm on my cheeks. Or my cheeks were warm, despite the wind.

I looked back and forth between the guys. You could taste the awkward.

"This shift is all about bad food and homework," I said to Brady.

Brady leaned in, and I forced myself to wrap my free arm around him to hug him good-bye. His lips moved against my ear. "Don't trust him. Call me later."

Mattie's hand tightened around mine.

"I will."

Chapter 27

Mattie. Only Mattie.

I told Mattie not to let on to Franklin and Greta what we were up to. Besides, I didn't think Franklin was speaking to me anyway after the pelting of rocks scene.

I gave Mattie the Windbreaker Brady had given me. It was too big anyway. We stopped off on the way home to get some face paint. I already saw the ballers with their blue-and-yellow faces and figured that many others would be following suit and would be the key to his camo at the bonfire.

"Just me and you, okay?" I said for probably the fifth time.

He nodded, still reading the label on the face paint. We were sitting on the floor next to my bed. Pinching,

I pulled tuft after tuft out of the area rug.

I reached out and snatched away the paint container from Mattie to gain back his attention. "Not Marilyn, not Brady, not Franklin. Right? Just us?" My voice hitched. Dammit. I was freaking.

Mattie took the paint back and set the container down on the carpet. He grabbed a hold of both my arms.

I got it. It's okay.

I nodded, even though it was far from okay. I closed my eyes and concentrated on the plan. "If we get the phone, it goes straight to the police. I'm not even completely sure it's going to be there. But it has to be." I felt sure it was there with my bracelet. But it wasn't like I could explain to him how I knew that. I opened my eyes to see his gaze moving over my face. Warmth spread through my chest.

The plan. I started my nervous talking again. "Maybe we should go together. No, we can't. Brady might follow me. I don't think he'll jump me or anything if I'm alone and he doesn't know I'm going for the phone. If we were together he'll know something was up—if he even is the killer. I can't be sure. I could be wrong about him and then the real killer is following me, or waiting for me at the school. But of course we need to go to the school. But if we—"

Just get to me. He jiggled my arms as he talked. *Get to the school.*

"I will."

Mattie's grip tightened on my arms and I was thankful for it.

Then he leaned in. I wasn't sure where the lean was headed, or maybe I knew exactly where, but I wasn't ready. Any more input and my head would explode.

I pulled away and got to my feet. "Okay. Seven o'clock. Meet me where the path empties out onto the football field. Far side of the woods. Then we'll backtrack together."

He answered by wrapping his arms around me. Just the balls of my feet were left on the carpet as he pulled me up into a hug. I wrapped my arms around his neck.

His voice in my head soothed me. I nodded along, my face pressed to his neck, as he reassured all my worries.

In and out of the woods. In and out. In and out. I chanted in my head. In and out of the woods and this would all be over.

Easy.

After Mattie left, I fished out the instant pics of me and Cooper from my pocket and tucked them in my jewelry box with dad. Clicking the cover closed, I smoothed my hand over the top of the box. They would be safe there. They could be together . . . in there . . . like an alternate ending of a choose-your-path adventure book. They could explore their happy-ever-after in a world where my dad was sorry. Where my dad was present. Ready to bring me to car shows and laugh at my jokes.

My phone buzzed.

Are you ok? It was Brady.

Yes I sent back.

buzzz **Should I come ober**. I assumed he meant "over" but I didn't want him ober or over.

No. Not feeling good

buzzz **Whats wrong**

I sighed. What excuse should I use? Cramps? Grouchy parents? You're my prime suspect and I don't feel like being killed today?

buzzz **Whats wrong**

Okay . . .

buzzz I flinched. **Whats wrong Cassie**

Im fine I sent.

This was getting fucking weird. He knew something. Something was wrong.

buzzz **See Eli today? Forgot to tell me. He said you going to bonfire. He was worried about you**

Crapsticks.

buzzz **Should i come ober**

My hands were shaking. **No**

"My stepdad is cleaning his guns," I mumbled under my breath. Instead I sent, **I dont want to play today. Call tomorrow.**

buzzz **Does Henry**

Why would he mention Henry? I stared at the phone as fear crept through me, and wondered where

Henry was when I last saw him. I ran across the hall to Henry's room. Empty. I shoved the curtain back and bumped my head against the window overlooking the backyard where Henry was sitting with his trucks after school. But he wasn't there now. Gone.

buzzz **Lets play with Henry**

I dropped my phone and ran downstairs into the living room. Henry? The TV was on. *SpongeBob.* I could see the front door was locked, but the room was empty. Henry? Where the fuck was Henry?

I found my voice. "Henry!"

I swung around toward the kitchen. "Henry!"

"What," a little voice said behind me.

I swung back toward the sound.

Henry sat forward on the couch where he had been slouched down and out of sight, looking back at me, unalarmed by the fever pitch of my voice. In two strides, I was in front of the couch scooping him into my arms. Henry tolerated it, patting my back gently.

"Arms, Henry. Hug with your arms," I told him.

Henry complied, putting the squeeze on me as I tried to breathe through the adrenaline.

Over his shoulder my mom was looking in from the kitchen with a wide-eyed stillness.

"Everything okay?" she asked.

I nodded and managed a smile as I released Henry. It was my biggest lie yet.

At dinner, I sawed into my meatballs with my knife as I visualized the path. The woods. Our spot. I kept going over the plan in my head until I could see my feet on the path and the curve of each tree.

"Cassie?" Mom's voice woke me from my thoughts. Mom and Landon were looking at me. Really looking at me. Their hands were clasped together loosely on the table, their meals untouched. Next to me, Henry was nibbling on a meatball stabbed on the end of his fork while humming. With all the cutting, my meatballs were reduced back to ground beef. I laid down my knife. I scooped up a mouthful with my fork and swallowed—not needing much chewing.

"Yeah?" I said, working to sound casual, but my voice came out in a whisper. I cleared my throat. I stabbed at three bow tie noodles. *Tink tink tink*, as my fork scraped against my plate. Eat. Eating was normal.

"You've been so different. Do you want to talk more about . . . anything?" Mom asked, her voice cracking at the end, and tears filled her eyes. Landon tightened his grip on her hand.

I froze, mashing my lips together as my eyes stung with tears. She was scared. Maybe she was scared of losing me, like I was afraid of losing people.

"I'm okay. Just a lot on my mind. Lot of shit—sorry, stuff—going on with Brady. And then everything with Gav. It's . . . hard."

She nodded violently. Talking. Talking about feelings was normal.

Her face still looked wild, but it was softening with relief. She was pressing forward against the table. Her shirt had a glob of sauce on top of the bump. Like a food catcher. It's not like she could lean any closer over her plate. It was the best she could do. She was doing the best she could. I watched her face again as she gave me a tight smile. She was trying. And not just for her shirt, or for the baby. She was trying to get closer to me.

I set down my fork. "I was thinking . . . Molly. For the baby. I vote Molly."

Mom and Landon blinked at me. Landon raised his fist and a smile broke slowly on his face. "Yes!"

Mom still looked gobsmacked.

I started up again before she could speak. I glanced at my arm where there was no watch. "I'm going to go to the bonfire tonight at school. It's Homecoming."

Her eyes widened and she nodded, her face softening even more. Socialization, I was sure, was another good sign for a depressed-seeming teen.

I didn't want her to worry. "Mom, maybe tomorrow we can get some lunch. The Flame has awesome burgers," I said, though the thought made my stomach clamp down.

The smile spread across her face. "I'd like that."

Tomorrow seemed far away. There was still so much to do.

Back in my room, I pulled my hair up in double pig-tail knots and used the blue hairspray I'd picked up at the drugstore. I wore my hoodie from school with dark pants and my black skater shoes from last year. This should be easy. Duck into the woods and get the phone. I made a deal to myself. I'd get my bracelet, give the cops the phone. No matter what the text said or who it led to. I picked my phone up off the carpet from where I had dropped it—no more messages from Brady—and slipped it into my pocket. My stomach ached. I wished I had skipped dinner.

In the hall, Henry was sitting outside my bedroom door, his head on his bent knees. I sat down next to him. "What's wrong, bud?"

"Nervous tummy," he said.

My hand froze where I was rubbing a hand over my own sick belly. "Why?"

"Do people get scared going out in the dark?" he asked.

"What people? Are you scared for me?"

He nodded.

"Aww. Dude, I'm fine," I told him. Maybe if I kept saying it, it would be true.

Henry looked up toward the light in the hall, or maybe it was the dust particles in the light beam. His shoulders loosened. "You won't be alone."

I thought of Mattie and I glanced at my phone.

Shit. Late.

I kissed Henry's temple. "No, I won't."

I pulled my hoodie forward to cover my hair. I made my way over to Snelling Ave., but turned the opposite direction of school toward the shops. I kept my strides long and glanced to my left. Guitar Land. Book Haven. Children's Paradise of the Lost Dolls. Guess they didn't get the memo of the two-word store names. I paused outside the Paradise and used the reflection to see behind me. Hard to tell if anyone was there.

I ducked inside Starbucks, did a show of looking over the specials after my eyes adjusted to the dim light, then weaved my way through the tables full of college people, old guys, and writer moms, and went down the hall past the bathrooms and out the rear door.

Outside again, I made a break through the alley and hopped the fence into someone's backyard, right through to the next street. I ran three houses down and did it again, making my way south and west. I made my way down Grover to Ivy and tried to stay in the shadow of the tree line. Across Ivy I ducked around the Quick-N-Shop building.

I took a sec to catch my breath and then peeked around the corner into the intersection I had just crossed.

Nothing. Not nothing—cars, two ten-year-olds on bikes, an old woman in a babushka—but not anyone coming at me with any sort of deadly weapon.

I walked the rest of the way along the A-frame houses on Grover, my skin buzzing with fear and anticipation. I could smell the smoke with still a block to go. It billowed over the tops of the trees, the sun setting to my right as I approached the path that would take me through the woods. Two people dressed in football jerseys were handing out pocket-size flashlights with the school logo.

"Woods are off-limits," they were repeating to everyone as they handed out the flashlights. As I reached for mine, I could already see the beams dancing off the trees ahead as a group made their way along the path.

I clicked mine on and started down the path. I pulled my phone from my pocket to check the time. Five minutes late and one power bar. Great. I sent off a text to Mattie that I was coming up on him in a minute. My phone beeped as I was pushing it into my pocket. I pulled it back out.

In the woods

That's . . . weird. I jumped at the *boom* of the bass drum as the band started up beyond the clearing ahead. A group approached me from behind. One of the guys was so into something he was saying he knocked into my shoulder, nearly toppling me.

"Sorry, sorry," he said as he stilled me with both hands on my arm. It was Eli. His eyes stayed on me as his hands slipped away and he kept step with his group who didn't seem to notice the encounter.

I got my bearings as to where I stood on the path. My entrance point to where I used to meet Cooper was behind me. I spun around and some girls gave me a strange look as I passed by them heading against traffic. I patted my pockets like I'd forgotten something.

I bent down to "tie my shoe" as a couple holding hands passed by. This would be it, my chance to slip away. As I was stepping off the path under the tree canopy, I heard a voice up the path.

"Hey!"

Someone had seen me. I ran. I clicked off the tiny beam of light bouncing around the trees and slowed my steps to listen. I could still hear the *boom boom, boom boom* of the bass and the horns chiming in. People cheering in that far-off kind of way. What I didn't hear was any breaking of branches or rustling of leaves that would give away someone coming up on me.

As I approached the stump where Cooper and I spent a few of our stolen afternoons, the hair on my arms stood on end. I shivered. Where was Mattie? Why would he wander in here alone, not knowing where he was going? We were supposed to meet and then go into the woods. I was the only one who knew where the phone was.

The only other landmark was where the body was found. It would be marked off in some way. More tape, I guessed. Cooper must have been running toward Snelling, which was straight—the most direct way out and to civilization.

I walked slowly, taking care with each step. A twig snapped under my shoe. I stopped. I pulled out my phone, turned up the volume, and checked the text again. The text was from Mattie's phone. My one power bar was flashing yellow.

I whipped off a text back:

Where are you?

I took one breath, then another and my phone chirped.

Keep coming

I held the phone in front of my face. My hand was shaking. None of this felt right. It didn't feel like Mattie on the other end of the text.

I swallowed. Brady could have followed Mattie instead of me. Could have been following him since after school when he was at my house. He probably knew all along what our plan was.

I looked around as if the shadows on the trees would give me the answers I needed. If Mattie was in trouble I needed to help him, but I also knew that I was walking into a trap. Would Brady hurt Mattie? Or me? Probably. I needed something to bargain with. I shivered again. I turned to look back, jerking in surprise as a drop hit my nose, then two more against my hand and forehead. I retraced my steps back to the log, my skin prickly as I slid my hand into the hollowed-out knot. I gasped as my fingers touched the smooth metal of the phone. My breath came out in little puffs. I thought it was going to be there, but didn't really know until that moment.

As my hand wrapped around it, I felt the ropiness of my bracelet bunched up around the middle. I pulled it toward me and stared at it. The cord was frayed. I unwrapped it from the phone.

The front of the phone was cracked in and I had to wipe away drops of moisture. I turned it over in my hands. The back was missing, but the SIM card was still there. Would it work after sitting in a damp log for this long? We had the same phone carrier. If Cooper's mom hadn't gotten around to canceling the service yet . . .

I got my fingernail under the SIM and slid it out. I blotted both sides on my T-shirt under my sweatshirt, leaning over to shelter it the best I could from the drizzle falling through the trees. Then I took out my own phone and swapped my SIM card for his. This essentially made my phone, his. Hitting the POWER button, I smiled as it sang to life. I pulled out my wallet, and the business card with the official-looking seal. I tapped off a quick text.

I wondered what Limey would think about getting a text from a dead boy.

Chapter 28

Before I reached them, I could hear choking and what sounded like a hissing. It sounded like some kind of animal. I could see bits of the yellow tape ahead through the trees and I quickened my steps, trying to watch ahead, but still trying to avoid falling on my face.

As I cleared the last oak, I had to flash my little flashlight around to take in what I was seeing. Mattie was on the ground three feet from me. He was writhing with jerks, and his face was pinched up and covered with sweat and had a huge swollen bruise over his right eye. The hissing and clicking was coming from Mattie, a victim who can't scream.

I felt frozen in place as I moved the narrow beam

down to see that his hands were clutching his leg. There was an angle between his knee and ankle where there shouldn't be one.

The breath caught in my throat and I must have taken a step because the voice to the right said, "Don't move."

I moved my light beam toward the sound to see Brady. His voice was low, a whisper almost. He was holding a rock the size of a melon above Mattie's head.

I held up a hand. "I'm not moving. I won't." I was surprised I had found my voice at all, let alone that it was almost steady, because it felt like one of those nightmares that if you screamed, nothing would come out. I glanced at Mattie. He had stilled. He lay with his elbows propped up behind him.

"Gimme your phone first," Brady said, tucking the rock under one arm.

I pulled out my phone from my back pocket and tossed it to him. He caught it with one hand and glared at me. He moved so that Mattie was between us. I guessed he was making sure I wouldn't make some kind of hero leap toward him.

He scrolled through my last sent text. "'Don't come to the bonfire. Raining here,'" he read. He looked up at me.

I shrugged. "My mom wanted to come meet me. I didn't want her to."

He nodded. "Do you have it? His phone?"

It bugged me that he couldn't even say his name.

"Whose, Cooper's?" I said.

His wandering eyes zeroed in on me, like he couldn't believe my sass.

"Yeah," I said, pulling it out to show him. "It's right here. What happens when I give it to you?" There was no way this scenario would come out sunshine and roses.

"Maybe you go get help and say that your 'friend,' had a bad accident fooling around in the woods."

"Let's keep it real. I'd tell them everything," I said.

Mattie hissed at me, but I ignored him.

"Why would they believe you? With me and the phone gone? Maybe I get Marilyn to alibi me. What's left but a few besties spouting lies in the rain?" Brady said.

"When did you start talking like a boy band?" I asked.

He wiggled his fingers toward me. "Give it to me."

I needed to stall. "I don't think Marilyn is as interested in keeping your secrets these days."

He shot a glance toward Mattie.

I raised my voice to keep his attention on me. "Was she ever, though? Was she spilling things about you to Cooper and Gobbers?" I asked.

He took two steps toward me. "You don't understand. What I had with Marilyn was real. Real is complicated. What she had with Cooper was poison. He was the one hurting her, sneaking around with you. You should know that."

I opened my mouth, but he cut me off.

"Come on, Cassie. Give it to me," he said. "I don't want to hurt you. Can't you see that I care for you?"

I threw the thought away before it caused the meatballs to come all the way back up. I glanced again at Mattie. I had to get Brady away from him. I slipped the phone into the front of my sports bra. "Come and get it." I turned and dodged right toward a large oak, then leaped over a bush. I felt like a superhero dodging and leaping until my foot snagged on a root and I went down. Hard. My flashlight flickered down to nothing. I threw it from me. I got about a two-second warning of footsteps on crunching branches. I spun onto my back, with my feet up, so when he dove for me I caught him with my feet, then launched him off again.

Unfortunately, he didn't launch far. I'd barely scrambled back to my feet before he'd recovered. He grabbed me in a bear hug from behind, pinning my arms. I went still. His lips moved next to my ear.

"Why? Why did you have to come here?" he said.

I stomped on his foot as hard as I could. In his surprise he loosened his grip just enough so I could get an elbow up swinging for his face. But I couldn't get enough rotation on it, and with a slight dodge of his head he avoided the blow. I jerked hard and managed to get us both toppling over, only I went down first with only his arm around me to break my fall.

It saved my face, but his weight pancaked me with the

ground, knocking the wind out of me. I felt him flip me over and his weight settled onto my stomach, but I was too distracted with the trying-to-breathe thing to notice the punch that came somewhere from my left. My head snapped right and my mouth exploded with pain. Blood seeped over my tongue.

He was screaming. "Stop fighting me! Give me the phone!"

"Fuck you, Brady!" I took a couple breaths. "Is this why Marilyn had all those bruises?"

Before he could answer, I swung my left hook up and connected with his temple, breaking the stem of his glasses. Lifting my hip, I used the momentum to throw him off me. I scrambled to get away. As soon as I felt his hand on my leg, I jabbed it back and hit something solid. I looked back and his nose was bleeding. I heard him groan in pain, but he still had my leg. I rolled onto my back and swung my other foot around and hit him in the face again. He let go with a string of nasally sounding curses.

With him caught off guard, my next kick landed between his legs. He curled up into a ball and groaned. "Why?" was about all I could make out.

I spit out a mouthful of blood. "You're asking me why? You tell me. Why did you kill Cooper?"

He took a couple more labored breaths before answering. "He was poisoning her. Marilyn. Just like he poisoned you."

"It was a lie! Eli told me. She was never with him."

I could see his eyes shining at me in the dark.

I could hear his brain. *Click Click Click.*

"She wasn't with him?" he asked.

"No. He didn't want her. He—"

He was on me then. Shaking me. "You lie. You fucking lie! I hate you and all your fucking lies!"

He slammed me down on the ground and his hands were on my throat. I clawed at his arms, and kicked and punched at him with any angle I could get. His eyes were wide and his whole body shook as his hands clamped tighter. The sky was changing colors. Red and blue flashes lit the night behind him.

I heard shouting, but everything was getting fuzzy and dark, like the whole world was running out of batteries. I felt something cool on my forehead and I turned my head just enough to see Cooper sitting next to me. No blood on his head. Just a beautiful glow of blond hair. "It's okay," he said. "They're coming."

Good, I thought. Whoever they were. Then Cooper slid his hand down over my eyes and everything went black.

Chapter 29

It would take time to get everything from the phone, but it didn't really matter. Not only had they caught Brady throttling a near lifeless me, after how angry I'd made him, he'd ranted for an hour and gave them everything they needed.

Five days later I was heading back into the hospital. I'd been discharged three days ago after only being in the hospital for two days. They couldn't find a reason to keep me longer. Even with bruises just about everywhere, there wasn't anything seriously wrong with me. Not that they didn't look. I had scans of every bone, tissue, and organ in my whole body. I was lucky, they said.

Ha. That's me, I told everyone, trying to keep the sarcasm from spoiling the moment.

Mattie was on the ninth floor. I pushed the button in the elevator. It was after visiting hours, but there was stuff that needed doing that couldn't wait. Headmaster Spanders had been all bugged about meeting with me ever since the article in the paper yesterday about the "heroes" that were "born in the woods behind the school." I mean, gross. Really? Why do we have to be born? Who writes that crap?

But Spanders was no fool. A spotlight had shone down on Saint Bernadette's and he wanted it lit as long as possible. Plus, my mom and stepdad told me they'd been getting nothing but advice from people about how the school owes us this or that. Like it was the school's fault a killer was enrolled there.

Spanders, or more likely his secretary, had whipped off a fancy letter informing me that the school board had granted me a full scholarship for my remaining years at St. B's. The letter also said that he was anxious to "christen" the moment with photos and a few reporters. Coffee and cookies to boot!

The elevator chimed, and after a quick look around, I strode out onto the ninth floor. ORTHOPEDICS the sign read in all its florescent glory. A nurse dressed in blue spotted me right off, but as she opened her mouth to say something, I lifted my chin a little higher to give her the full view of my face, which included the added bonus of bruises that ran all wicked down my neck.

Whatever words she had got stuck. She knew me. Or of me. She closed her mouth into a smile and looked away.

I'd been getting that a lot lately. Smiles. And staring. I was starting to understand the staring, people interested in the so-called fame. But the smiles? The smiles were harder to figure out. People at school who had never bothered before said hi and other friendly things. I asked Eli about it. "Why do they like me? All I did was save Gav. They hated Gav."

"Yeah," he said. "But you also fought for Cooper."

I didn't know what to think about all that, and I still don't. But I wasn't going to let an opportunity go to waste. I entered the meeting with Spanders with a super smile of my own, and brought with me an agenda. Part of me wanted to leave the whole Saint Bernadette's thing behind, chuck second semester and go back to being me at Kellogg Senior High.

But in a way I felt proud. That I could walk down the hall yesterday at school and just be me. Hair up, slouching, or whatever. Even in a St. B's uniform, who I was didn't have to be a secret anymore.

I also realized that I wasn't going back without Mattie. He was as smart as me or smarter. He risked his life and was hurt way more than me, all for a boy he didn't even know. At least that's how I told it to Spanders. I know Mattie was there for me. And I couldn't stand to not be there for him. He'd never left me. Even when I wandered away from him as far as I had ever gone. He risked his life for me, and thankfully managed to not die.

I gave the door of room 9408 a nudge with my elbow. It swung open without a creak. The ledge by the window was packed with boys. Well, two boys: Gav and Franklin. I glanced down at Mattie, who was sleeping as I made my way over to them.

Every time I saw Mattie's leg, it gave me the heebies. No joke. There were pins and pulleys that were hooked to actual weights hanging from the end of his bed. Mattie had been pretty doped the last two times I was here. Which was fine, really. No sense in dealing with that kind of pain . . . until you had to.

I leaned down to hug Franklin first. His arms stayed at his sides, a silent protest maybe. He had managed to avoid me since the night of the bonfire, which was an impressive sulk for a couple of rocks thrown at his mom's van, considering I'd almost died. I felt like I could use that fact against him.

"I almost died, you know," I said with effort. My vocal cords were still bruised from the throttling Brady gave me.

He left his arms limp, but hooked his chin over my shoulder. "I know. Why do you think I've been so mad?" I squeezed him tighter.

Gav was already bouncing on the balls of his feet when I finally broke away from Franklin. Unlike

Franklin, Gav had been anxious to see me since he was released. Visiting me in the hospital was his first stop, even before home. Well, not his first stop. That was McDonald's, but at least he'd thought to grab me a burger.

When Gav was finished smashing me in a hug, he kept his arms around me, leaning back only far enough to look me over. "How are you?"

"Same as last time you saw me."

He tipped his chin toward Mattie's sleeping form. "Don't suppose you're going to let him outta reach once he's out of here?"

"I think the feeling is going to be pretty mutual."

Twisting out of his hold avoiding any more questions of double meanings, I reached over to pinch Franklin's arm. "You still with Greta?"

That had Franklin smirking. "Yup."

"Shh!" Gav hit his pointer against his mouth sharply. "We don't speak of such things."

We chatted for a bit, then I watched as they gathered up their boards and bags.

"Leaving?" Though it was obvious.

"Yeah," Gav said, and he didn't ask if I was staying, because I guess that, too, was obvious. "But we'll see you. Yeah?"

"I know," I said. Because I would. We might not be skating soon, and we might not be going to the same school, but the separations, the ones life (and death) threw at us, were temporary. The only real road blocks were the ones I put up myself. I was working on tearing them down.

After they left, I moved back to Mattie's side.

Mattie's mom wasn't there, but she must have been recently. I could still smell her jasmine tea bags. There was a banana nut muffin, the kind that came wrapped in cellophane from vending machines. Those things were da bomb. In magic marker she had written my name. No, Mattie had written my name. *Cass.* Just Cass.

I sat down in the chair that had been vacated by Mattie's mom. The rail on that side was still let down. When I took his hand, his eyes opened.

Hi.

"Hi," I whispered back. "You're an idiot. You know? It's going to be weeks until you heal."

He shrugged me off.

I stared him down until he gave me a wincing grin. "Whatever. Can't work on tre flips until spring anyways," I said, my voice cracking to nothing at the end.

I wanted to tell Mattie how my mom, and even Landon, had cried at the ER that night and said all the things they should have been saying for a long time, and how I didn't even give them a hard time or make them feel guilty. And that I said all the right things back. I wanted to know if Marilyn had been by, and if any of the flower bundles were from her. But really I was just so damn happy to be here with my friend, my Mattie, that none of that seemed to matter.

I lay my head down on the bed and let the tears come. Let is a deceiving word, since there wasn't shit I could do about it. I cried until I had to mop my face with my free sleeve.

It was stupid. Crying in front of him like this. It must be like some kind of Chinese torture for him to be trapped with female drama. But as I stood and tried to leave, he gripped my hand tighter. His face was pinched tight and his eyes were wet. My heart jumped, thinking he was in pain. But then I heard him clearer than I ever had.

Stay. Stop running away.

I sank back into the chair, my heart hammering in my chest. "Okay."

He bent his arm, pulling me closer. He curled my hand up to his mouth, and placed a kiss to the side of my wrist next to my bracelet. I set my head down on his arm.

Don't leave.

"Never."

ACKNOWLEDGMENTS

First big ups to my agent, Barbara Poelle, who believed in this book, and in me, and who always has my back. She's the one I'd want as my second in a drag race or bar fight. Or really, I'd just cower behind her while she battles the ninjas and zombies for me, because that's what a good agent does.

Wild applause for my editor, Marlo Scrimizzi, who seemed to know these characters and this story as well as I did, and always wanted to know more. She was the Miyagi to my Daniel-san. She asked all the right questions and helped me find the heart of this story.

Cheers! To my first critique partners Bob Hussey and Alex Liuzzi who, although not YA writers themselves, not only put up with, but enthusiastically discussed teen angst and crushes and made me, for the first time, feel like a REAL WRITER. As an add-on to that, my very first writing instructor Mart Gardner at the Loft, who was the first person in the literary world who said, "You can write!" not as permission, but validation.

To lovely family and friends who have been supportive of the dream and especially to those who read painfully rough, early work and still offered support! And to the professional writers/editors/agents along the way who gave feedback, advice, and encouragement.

To the numerous writers (both pre and post published) whom I've met at conferences, workshops, online classes, and social media who inspire me, support me, and remind me that we are not alone in this journey—and really, who have made, and continue to make, this journey loads of fun!

To my FOREVER critique partner Kip Wilson, who is always there to make me laugh, dry my tears, and hold the virtual barf bag when needed. She is a star.

And lastly, but not leastly, to my family. My children: Wyatt, Nick, and Alice. Thank you for putting up with my writing-related distractions and absence, and knowing that you three come first in my heart. Never be afraid to make big goals and chase them tirelessly. And to my husband Dan: my real-life love story. My muse. My tireless supporter of whims and dreams and crazy optimism, and endless fangirling—none of which he fully understands but supports because he is amazing like that.

And finally, thanks to YOU, dear reader, for coming on this journey with me!

MONICA ROPAL lives in friendly St. Paul, Minnesota, with her husband and three children— whom she lovingly refers to as her three-ring circus. In addition to writing and playing ring-master, Monica also works as a hospice nurse. You can visit her at monicaropal.com and on Twitter @MonicaYAwriting.